THE JILTED BILLIONAIRE GROOM

JENNIFER YOUNGBLOOD

ARBOR
HOUSE

GET YOUR FREE BOOK

Get Beastly Charm: A Contemporary retelling of beauty & the beast as a welcome gift when you sign up for my newsletter. You'll get information on my new releases, book recommendations, discounts, and other freebies.

Get the book at:

http://bit.ly/freebookjenniferyoungblood

CHAPTER 1

Finley's heart jumped into overdrive when he saw the roomful of women with their practiced smiles and watchful eyes—well-groomed vultures—gathered around tables in the banquet room. His mom had invited him to have lunch with her at the country club. As they were entering the café, she took a detour that led them here. "Please tell me this is not what I think it is." It was bad enough to be humiliated by Emerson on national TV when she declared her love for Titan's football quarterback Riker Dylan and then ran off with him. Finley didn't need this to add to it.

Fiona raised her chin. "It's time for you to quit dinking around. You need to find a good woman, so you can stop the pity party and get on with your life." She pointed to the room. "Those women are beautiful, accomplished ... everything you could ever want. Finley, I'm sure that even you can find a contender out of Dallas's finest."

He threw his hands in the air. "Why do you care who I date, Mom?"

Her eyes bore into his as she stepped closer and lowered her voice. "Because you're my son, and I care about you." She brushed her hand over her silk shirt as if to smooth the wrinkles. There were none, however. As usual, Fiona Landers was the picture of perfection. "This self-pity routine has to stop," she continued through clenched teeth. "You need to find a suitable companion and settle down. Your dad's not getting any younger, and the business is taking its toll on him."

Finley's heart clutched. "Is Dad okay?" There'd been a cancer scare a year ago—a brain tumor, but it was benign. A surgeon had removed it, and his dad was back to work before the week's end.

"Kenton's fine," Fiona said with a flourish of her hand. "I want the two of us to start traveling more."

"You want me to take over the bulk of running the business," he finished.

"Exactly. If you can prove to your dad that you're capable of running the business, then maybe he won't mind stepping away from the helm occasionally."

He laughed in disbelief. "And finding a woman is going to somehow magically achieve this? I already run a large portion of the business. Who do you think was instrumental in developing the software that's revolutionizing the agriculture industry?" He pointed to his chest. "Me. Dad's a workaholic. Even if I lived at the office, he still wouldn't step away from work."

"Don't turn this around to make it a thing about your dad. This is about you and finding the right woman," she said stiffly. "Since you were reluctant to take the lead, I decided to do it for you."

His voice rose. "And what? I'm just supposed to waltz in there and pick one? Seriously?"

A rustle went through the room as the women looked toward him. A few smiled and waved. One even winked like they were sharing an inside joke.

"Don't be a sour puss," Fiona commanded, nudging his arm. "Smile at them. They're here to see you."

It was all Finley could do to force a smile.

"The plan is for you to interview them—two to three minutes each. Pick your top five and go on dates. It shouldn't be hard to weed them out from there."

Had he not seen the serious expression on his mom's face, Finley would've thought this whole thing was some crazy comedy setup. The kind where at the end, the person says, *Smile, you're on camera. Gotcha!* He didn't know whether to laugh or cry. "I guess I deserve this for what I did to Emerson," he said quietly. Karma was having a heyday with this one.

Fire sparked in Fiona's eyes. "Don't speak that vile girl's name. She's the reason we're dealing with this in the first place. If she hadn't gone berserk, you'd be married by now, and all of this would be behind us."

"I hardly think Emerson choosing the man she loved was going berserk, Mom."

Her eyes rounded in disbelief. "Now you're siding with her?"

"I'm not siding with anyone." A pit settled in his stomach as he eyed his mom. "I'm not going in there. I'll remain single 'til the day I die before I subject myself to such humiliation."

She rocked back, blinking fast as she touched her short hair. "Everything is in place," she stammered. "All you have to do is go in there and have lunch. Afterwards, you can talk to them." She smoothed his collar, giving him an encouraging smile as she patted his shoulder. "Those women are clamoring for you. Just be yourself."

He frowned, his stomach knotting as he slung out the words. "They're not clamoring for me, they're here because they want to hitch their wagons to the Landers' name. It's all about the money and notoriety. It has nothing to do with me."

"Don't be ridiculous," she laughed nervously. "You are a Landers, and there's nothing you can do to change that. The women in that room were put through a thorough screening process to ensure they're worthy of you."

An incredulous laugh rose in Finley's throat. "You screened them?"

She gave him a funny look. "Of course, why wouldn't I? It's your future we're talking about. You can just as easily fall in love with a woman of good breeding as you can a nobody. We're just stacking the deck for success."

Although Finley was standing right in front of his mom, he felt like they were oceans apart. *This is insane!* He clenched his jaw. "I won't do it." He shook his head. "You've gone too far this time." He motioned. "You can just march in there and tell them the charade is over."

Fiona's face fell. "Why're you being so unreasonable?" Tears gathered in her eyes as her voice quivered. "Can't you see that I'm trying to help you?" She leaned closer, lowering her voice. "We need a win here, Finley. We need to show the world that you've moved past Emerson."

"I have moved past her, Mom. I sure as heck don't need another woman on my arm to prove that."

Her face drained, tears rolling down her cheeks. "I've put weeks of planning into this. Happiness can be found right inside that room." She shook her head. "I don't understand why you're being so obstinate about this."

Panic fluttered inside Finley. Had his mom jumped up and down and cursed him, he could've held his ground. But the one thing he couldn't tolerate was seeing her cry. He felt like a battering ram was crushing his insides as he touched her arm. "I didn't mean to upset you."

Her lower lip trembled. "I just wish you'd step outside yourself long enough to see that this thing with Emerson didn't just affect you. It's a blight on our entire family. I'm trying to fix it the best way I know how."

He blew out a defeated breath. Perhaps his mom's intentions were good, even though they were sorely misguided. The easiest way to solve this was to just go in there and put on a good face—get the blasted thing over with. "Fine. I'll do it," he muttered.

"You will?"

"Yeah." He felt sick.

She brushed away her tears and rewarded him with an appreciative look. "Thank you." She patted his arm, offering a wan smile. "I have a good feeling about this. The girl for you is in there." She squared her chin. "I know it." She took in a breath, touching her face. "Is my makeup okay?"

"You look beautiful," he replied mechanically.

"Hello," a cheery voice boomed.

Dede Chambers, Emerson's friend strode toward them in six-inch heels and a short, red sundress that showcased her tan, toned legs. She flashed a warm smile at Fiona like they were the best of friends. "Hello, Mrs. Landers."

Fiona smiled brightly, giving Finley a look that said, *See, you should listen to me more often.* "Dede. I'm glad you could make it."

Dede wrinkled her nose. "Sorry, I'm late. Traffic was a beast." She hugged Fiona, air-kissing her on both cheeks. Then she turned to Finley, the corners of her lips tipping in a mischievous smile. "There's the man of the hour. How are you?"

"Good," he clipped. Dede had called several times over the past few weeks. They'd had a few conversations, made vague plans to get together sometime. No doubt Dede was beautiful with a Barbie doll figure and stylish-blonde hair, but there was a predatory glint in her eyes that turned him off. Dede was just like all the other women crowded in that room—a beautiful package with a litany of polite society catch-phrases rolling off her tongue, but no real substance. He'd been drawn to Emerson because she was real. He'd trade the whole kit and caboodle of the vultures in that room for one down-to-earth woman who loved him for him, not for his money or influence.

A stunning brunette emerged from the room, her carriage radiating confidence. "Hi, I'm Celeste Hendricks," she said in a cultured, husky voice. Her hopeful eyes held Finley's. "I saved you a seat next to me."

Dede's eyebrow arched as she stepped close to Finley, linking her arm through his. "I'm afraid that won't work," she said smoothly, her lips easing into an apologetic smile. "Finley's sitting with me during the luncheon."

The brunette thrust out her lower lip in a petulant pout. "That's too bad," she purred. She touched his free arm, running a manicured nail over his skin. "I guess I'll just have to put my allotted interview time to good use. See ya inside," she winked. She cut her eyes at Dede, flashing a malevolent expression, before turning on her heel and strutting back into the room.

Finley's skin crawled, and he longed to escape. No way could he handle being in the middle of all those fawning women cat-fighting over him. Fiona must've realized he was on the verge of losing it because she laughed lightly, taking Dede's arm and pulling her away from Finley. "Let's take things one step at a time, shall we?" She gave Dede a warning look. "You'll get your time, just like everyone else, dear."

Amusement flickered in Dede's eyes. "I'm counting on it," she said softly, holding Finley's gaze until he looked away.

Fiona lifted her chin. "Shall we go in? It's past time for the luncheon to start."

Finley coughed. "You go. I'll be right behind you. I will," Finley reiterated when he saw Fiona's face tighten. "Five minutes is all I ask."

For a second, Fiona looked like she might argue but finally nodded. "Okay, five minutes," she said firmly. "If you're not seated by my side, I'm coming after you."

"Got it," he clipped, saluting.

As he watched his mom and Dede go into the room, he made a split-second decision. No way was he going in there. Fiona sat down at the front center table, but her eyes remained glued on him like she was ready to spring up from her seat any second. If he outright fled, she'd run after him and play on his sympathies until she persuaded him to stay. Waiters buzzed past him, carrying platters of salads and rolls.

The time to act was now!

"Hey." He reached out and touched a waiter on the sleeve. The guy stopped, a surprised expression coming over his face. Finley sized him up. Early twenties, hair pulled back in a man bun. There was a grungy aura about the guy—the perfect candidate for what he had in mind.

"Yeah? What is it?"

"How would you like to make an easy thousand bucks?"

Interest lit the guy's eyes. "I'm listening."

"There's an older woman sitting at the front table. Don't look," Finley quickly cautioned before the guy could turn around, "she's watching us. I want you to create a distraction that will keep her preoccupied."

Wariness seeped into the guy's eyes. "What's the catch?"

"No catch." Finley moved so that the waiter blocked his mom's view. He reached in his pocket and pulled out a wad of cash. Quickly, he thumbed through it, counting out a thousand and placing it in the guy's hand. "The distraction needs to be big enough to keep the ladies occupied for a few minutes."

The waiter looked down at the money in his palm. "Make it two grand, and you've got a deal."

Finley's jaw tightened. "Really? All you have to do is one simple thing, man."

"Yeah, and that one simple thing could get me fired. So, what'll it be? Do you want a distraction or not?"

"Fine." He counted out another grand and slapped it down in the guy's palm.

The guy grinned, shoving the money into his pocket. "You just bought yourself a mega-sized distraction. Nice doing business with you, Mr. Landers."

Finley flinched slightly at the use of his last name. *Duh.* Of course, the waiter knew who he was. He was lucky he got off paying a couple grand.

As the waiter strolled away, Finley held his breath, mentally crossing his fingers. Minutes later, there was a loud crash, followed by his mom's shriek of outrage. The waiter had "stumbled" and dumped the entire tray of salads on his mom and the ladies sitting next to her.

For an instant, Finley's feet were frozen to the floor as he watched the scene play out. Fiona looked down at the ranch dressing trickling down the front of her silk shirt. Rage twisted her features as she turned her venom on the waiter. Yep, the poor guy would get sacked, for sure. After Fiona clawed his eyes out.

Go now! his mind screamed.

Not looking back, Finley made a break for it. He wasn't sure where he was going, but it would be somewhere far away from here.

Ashley took a bite of cereal as she looked across the table at her nephew Ian. It had been a long, challenging week trying to keep him occupied while she juggled projects at work. This week, of all weeks, was not the best time to try and entertain a precocious ten-year-old. Especially with the new design account she'd just landed—a trendy condominium complex just outside of downtown Ft. Worth. Her phone buzzed. It was her boss Jill. She sighed and hit the side button to silence it. She'd call Jill on the drive into work.

"When are we going to the zoo?" Ian asked eagerly.

"We talked about this, remember? We're going as soon as we get finished at my office. I have a meeting with my boss."

"I know. To go over plans for the condo." He rolled his eyes.

"Yes, that's right," she barked, then let out a long sigh. It wasn't Ian's fault she was slammed at work. She'd dragged poor Ian to scores of appointments and meetings this week. He'd grumbled about it, as any kid would. But all in all, he'd done better than she'd expected. Thank goodness for iPads and video games!

His face fell, along with his shoulders as he dropped his spoon against the bowl with a loud ping.

He was so darn cute with his bright blue eyes, shock of thick, scraggly red hair, and freckles. She wished she could drop everything and take him to the zoo this very minute, but it just wasn't possible. She'd worked her whole career for a chance like this and couldn't drop the ball now when things were starting to click. "Hey, I promise. One short meeting, and then we'll go to the zoo."

She gave him a pleading look. In response, he folded his arms over his chest, thrusting out his lower lip. "Afterwards, we'll get pizza and ice cream," she added.

"Really?" A wide smile curved his lips as his demeanor changed —an iceberg melting before her very eyes.

"Really."

"Yeah!" he shouted, punching a fist in the air. He sprang to his feet and started dancing as he made beatbox sounds with his mouth like a rapper.

She laughed, shaking her head. How one kid could have so much energy was beyond her. She'd nicknamed him Taz for the Tasmanian Devil character in old Looney Tunes cartoons.

He stopped the song as suddenly as he'd started it. "Hey, can I call my mom?" He sat back down in his seat and shoved a large spoonful of cereal in his mouth.

"Sure." Hopefully, they'd be able to reach her this time. She'd been trying to call Lexi for two days. The nagging feeling that something was wrong grew stronger by the day. Two weeks ago, Lexi called out of the blue asking if she could watch Ian for a few days, while she worked through some problems with her boyfriend Nolan. Considering it was Nolan Webb they were talking about, there was no telling what was going on. Nolan owned a string of casinos in Vegas and was about as shady as they came. From the first minute Lexi hooked up with him, Ashley feared no good would come of it. But Lexi was head over heels in love with Nolan and wouldn't listen to reason.

Ashley picked up on the desperation in Lexi's voice when she called about her watching Ian. Even though it was terribly inconvenient, Ashley didn't have the heart to tell her older sister *no*. Lexi had been so good to her over the years. She owed her everything. A few short hours after the conversation, Lexi put Ian on a plane by himself to Dallas. A few days turned into two weeks, and now Lexi wasn't answering her phone or returning texts. Something was wrong!

She dialed Lexi's number and put it on speaker. It went straight to voicemail.

"Why's Mom not answering, Aunt Ashley?"

The worry on Ian's face caused her gut to churn. "I'm not sure." Did Ian know something? She rolled the words around in her head, trying to figure out a way to ask Ian questions without alarming him. "Is everything okay between your mom and Nolan?" It was a stupid question, really. Things had never been okay between Lexi and Nolan. Ashley suspected there was abuse taking place, but Lexi didn't want to admit it.

Ian shrugged, a shadow coming over him. "I guess."

Ian knew something he wasn't telling. She could see it in his eyes.

The doorbell rang.

"Maybe it's Mom." Ian jumped up to answer it.

Ashley stood. "Hold your horses. I'll get it." Was it Lexi? Had she not answered her phone so she could surprise them? She looked through the peephole, disappointed it was the mailman instead of her sister. She opened the door.

"Hi, Ashley," the elderly man said.

"Hey, Steve," she responded mechanically, forcing a polite smile.

He handed her a large padded envelope. "This wouldn't fit in the mailbox," he explained, "so I figured I'd better bring it to you."

"Thanks," she murmured as she said goodbye and closed the door. There was no return address, but she could tell from the postage that it had been mailed from Las Vegas.

Ian stepped up and peered over her shoulder, tugging on her arm. "What is it?"

"I'm not sure. Grab me a butter knife from the kitchen, would ya? So I can open it."

"Yep." In a flash, Ian was back with the knife.

Ashley sat down at the kitchen table, cut open the top, and pulled out the contents of the envelope. She gasped when she saw the stacks of money, passports, social security cards, and a driver's license. She picked up the license. Her throat went dry as she swallowed. It was her picture with the name Sunny Day, and it had an address in Montana. Confusion swirled through her as she opened the passports. Sunny Day and Ian Day.

Ian reached for a stack. "Money!" he chimed with glee.

She blocked his hand. "Wait a minute. Don't touch it." This couldn't be good. She opened the note. She glanced to the bottom. It was from Lexi.

Hey, Sis.

As I'm writing this letter, I hope it'll never be sent. I hope that instead, I'll be the one greeting you and that all will be well. If you do get this package, it means that things didn't work out as I'd hoped. There were things going on with Nolan that I couldn't tell you about over the phone. Ian saw something he shouldn't have, and I fear he may be in danger. As soon as I seal this package and drop it off to a trusted friend, I'm going to talk to Nolan in the hope that I can make him understand that Ian is just a child who won't pose a threat. I can convince Ian to remain quiet about what he saw. He's probably already forgotten it by now.

I'm sure if I were standing before you, I'd get a lecture on my not-so-great choice in men. Please don't judge me, Ash. Nolan certainly has his faults, but I love him heart and soul. I need him in my life. There's goodness in him, I know it! I'm sure it's hard for you comprehend needing anyone. You've always been the strong one—so focused and determined to accomplish your goals. You make me proud, Sis. It's comforting to know that if anything should happen to me, Ian will be under your care.

Like I said, if you do receive this package, it means my love for Nolan couldn't save me in the end. You must get out of there immediately. Go where no one knows you—some place you've never been before, where Nolan won't think to look. Take the cash and ID's. Leave everything else behind. Whatever you do, don't tell anyone where you're going and don't use credit cards, or he'll find you. I'm sorry, Sis, to lay this burden on you. What I would give to see Ian once more. Please tell him that Mommy loves him with all her heart. He's the one bright spot—my best achievement!

May God be with you both. I'm truly sorry to put you in this situation. Please take care of Ian. You're his only hope.

I love you!
    Lexi

P.S. You've always been my ray of sunshine, but you're far too serious for your own good. Hopefully, your new name will be a good reminder that life is to be savored and enjoyed, not just something to check off a list.

Ashley clutched her chest and gulped in a strangled breath, tears burning her eyes. *No! It can't be!* A silent prayer rose in her heart. *Please let Lexi be alive!* She couldn't imagine a world without her free-spirited sister who saw the world through rose-colored glasses.

Her lower lip trembled as she tried to hold back the sob in her chest.

"What's wrong?" Ian asked.

Her hands shook as she dropped the note and reached for her laptop. She typed in a search for *Lexi Reed* and *Las Vegas*. It didn't yield anything about Lexi, so she added *The Paradise* Nolan's largest casino in with the other phrases.

Former Showgirl and Musical Sensation Found Dead in Hotel Room of Heroin Overdose was the first thing that came up on a local news outlet. When she saw Lexi's name a few sentences later, she couldn't hold back the tears. She heard Ian speak and realized that he'd read the note. His face crumpled, tears rolling down his cheeks. "No!" He fell to his knees, sobbing. Somehow, she managed to make her legs comply with the directive to stand up as she went to him and flung her arms around him. "No!" he repeated over and over, trying to push her away, but she held him tight. "Nolan killed her," he wailed.

A sense of horror overtook Ashley as she gave way to the sob building in her chest, grief convulsing out of her in ragged gasps.

After her tears were spent and Ian's weeping waned to muffled, intermittent sniffs, the full scope of their situation hit Ashley with enough force to nearly take her breath away. Nolan Webb knew where she lived, probably knew that she had Ian. His goons could show up here any minute.

They had to get out of here—fast!

CHAPTER 2

Two months later ...

The smell of cedar invaded Finley's senses as he rested his head against the back of the sauna, willing his body to relax. The heated conversation he'd had with his mom a few hours earlier was still playing through his mind like the wrong note in a repetitive song. Sometimes it stunk to be an only child because he got one hundred percent of his mom's attention. *Lucky me.* He pulled a face ... *not!* The woman was smothering him. Finley didn't know which his mom was the most ticked about—him fleeing the country club or the fact that he took the family jet to Europe for a month and a half. He'd spent a week in Paris, two in Italy, and three in a small village in Southern Germany. The time away from Dallas helped give him added perspective on the situation. Plus, it had been wonderful to go somewhere where no one knew him. He was just another face in the crowd.

The more he thought about that ridiculous scenario at the country club, the more he came to believe it was karma—his payback for attempting to force Emerson to marry him. Right after Emerson left with Riker, Finley's world came crashing down. Now he realized that he and his family had been in the wrong. Love was something that couldn't be bought, and it sure as heck couldn't be forced. He'd written Emerson a long email, telling her how sorry he was for the part he played in the debacle. She responded back saying all was forgiven and that she still considered him a good friend. Then she went on for three more paragraphs telling him how happy she and Riker were. At the end, she expressed hope that he would one day find the right girl for him.

The right girl. He let out a long breath. Was she truly out there? He wanted to find the right one, but how? He had to get it right this time. His heart couldn't handle another mistake. He rubbed his neck to relieve some of the tension.

After leaving Europe, Finley decided he wasn't ready to go back to Dallas in late August when it was as hot as Hades, so he came here to the hotel his family owned in Park City, Utah where he was staying in the penthouse suite. The weather was pleasant, and in another couple of week, the leaves would start to turn. It was the perfect place to decompress and clear his head. While his mom was ticked, his dad found the situation amusing. "You're a grown man and can go wherever you want. Just make sure you don't fall behind on your work," Kenton warned.

The software arm of the business was taking off like wildfire. Scores of farms across the US were clamoring to implement the program, which was fantastic; but it also required a lot of manpower to keep everything running smoothly. They'd gotten several offers from large conglomerates to purchase the software, but the plan was to hold onto it for now. It was all Finley could do to stay on top of everything. He'd fallen a little behind in Europe, but had been working long hours the past couple of weeks since coming to Park City. He was almost caught up. This evening, he planned to have dinner at the hotel restaurant and then veg in his room—maybe even go for a late-night swim. Tomorrow morning, he'd get an early workout, then put in seven or eight hours before taking the rest of the day off. No matter how hard he worked, there was always more to do. Finley had no intention of becoming a workaholic like his dad. Life was too short to spend every waking second worrying about the company.

Even as the thought entered his mind, he laughed at himself. Here he was, supposedly relaxing, and his mind was ticking through all the work items that still needed to be done. *So much for not being a workaholic.* Finley let out a long sigh as he stood and wrapped his towel tighter around his waist. As he stepped out of the sauna, a flash of movement caught his attention. "You can't be in here. This is a private area." He made a mental note to remind the hotel manager that this space was off-limits for the other guests. He glanced at the bench where his clothes were and caught a blur of red hair as his mind registered what was happening. A kid was rummaging through the pockets of his shorts!

"What do you think you're doing?" he demanded.

The boy froze, his eyes turning to saucers as he grabbed the shorts and took off running.

"Hey!" he yelled, sprinting across the room after the kid. "Stop!" Finley caught the boy's arm before he could exit the door. "You can't just barge into a private area and go through my shorts!"

Fear streaked through the kid's eyes as he looked up at Finley. His lower lip trembled. "I'm sorry, Mister. I didn't mean any harm. I was just looking for some change to get a drink. Please don't tell my aunt. She'll kill me."

"Where's your aunt?"

"Working," he stammered.

Finley's eyebrows darted together. "Where does she work?"

"Here, in the hotel." The door opened as a middle-aged, bald man stuck his head in the door. Good timing. It was Drake Bradford, the hotel manager, just the man Finley wanted to speak to.

"Forgive me for interrupting you sir," Drake said timidly, "but I happened to be walking by and heard yelling." His eyes went to the boy. "Is everything okay?"

Finley realized he was still clutching the boy's arm. He released him, feeling a smidgen of guilt when he saw the red indents from his fingertips against the boy's fair skin. "This thief was going through my shorts." He shot the boy a withering look. "Do you know where his aunt is? I'd like to have a word with her."

The manager looked puzzled. "Do you mean his mom?"

"Yeah," the boy said quickly, his face turning as red as his hair. "My mom. That's what I meant."

There was something odd going on here. Why had the boy first called the woman his aunt and now his mom? Was the little weasel having fun at his expense?

"I'll get Miss Day right away." Drake scowled at the boy. "We'll get to the bottom of this," he said briskly, hurrying away.

Finley motioned to a nearby bench. "You might as well sit down as we wait, and don't even think of making a run for it," he warned when the boy eyed the open door.

The boy sighed heavily, his shoulders sagging. "Fine." He thrust the shorts at Finley, then shuffled over and sat down on the bench. Finley stood, holding the shorts, not sure what to do. If he went to a dressing room to put on the shorts, the boy would most likely flee. Then again, would it really hurt if the boy left? Finley only had ten dollars in his shorts. In retrospect, he probably should've just let the kid take the money. The kid looked pitiful sitting there dejected, like he'd lost his best friend. Finley hadn't exactly been an angel at that age. He couldn't pass judgment on the kid. It'd been a shock seeing the kid in the private area, and he'd reacted. Then again, if the boy was trying to steal from him, chances were, he'd steal from hotel guests as well. It was probably better to just nip it in the bud here and now.

The boy sat staring down at the floor.

"What's your name?"

Silence.

"I asked your name," Finley repeated more firmly.

"Ian."

"How old are you?"

Ian glanced at him, then back down at the floor. "Ten." He squeaked out the word as if it were a question.

"Aren't you supposed to be in school?" It was late August. Surely school had already started here.

"I'm home schooled." He scuffed his feet back and forth against the floor, sitting on his hands.

What kind of woman was so irresponsible that she let her kid run wild around a hotel while she worked? An unsupervised kid was bound to get into trouble. The fault lay mainly with the woman, Finley decided.

A few minutes later, Drake returned with a slender, dark-haired woman dressed in a maid uniform. The second she stepped through the door, she rushed to Ian's side. "What did you do?" she seethed.

"I was just thirsty and looking for money for the drink machine," he stammered.

"This is unacceptable. We'll talk about it later," she muttered. "I'm so sorry about this," she began as she turned. Then she stopped, cocking her head in surprise. "Fin?"

Finley's heart skipped a beat. Even dressed in a uniform, the woman was strikingly beautiful. Her dark lustrous hair was pulled back in a simple ponytail, emphasizing her large almond-shaped eyes and high cheekbones. It then registered that she'd called him by name. "Do we know each other?" He searched his brain. Had they met before? She had a slight Southern accent, but the boy didn't. Had he met her in Texas, or was it here? There was something vaguely familiar about her. Why wasn't it coming to him? A woman like her would be hard to forget.

"Miss Day, I hardly think *Fin* is an appropriate way to address the owner of this hotel," Drake snipped, his eyes looking up at the ceiling, causing his forehead to bubble into loose wrinkles. "It's Mr. Landers to you."

The slightest hint of color tinged her cheeks as she blinked rapidly, clasping her hands together. "Of course. I meant no disrespect."

"It's okay," Finley said smoothly, holding up a hand to Drake as he gave her an apologetic smile. Drake had called her Miss versus Mrs. Did that mean she was single?

Drake eyed the woman. "Your son broke into an area clearly marked *Private* and tried to steal money from Mr. Landers' shorts. I've been lenient on you, Miss Day, have allowed the boy to come with you to work since you're a single mom with no one to watch him." His eyes darted to Finley like he feared he might've said too much. Finley kept his expression placid. Drake turned his attention back to the woman. "You assured me that Ian would stay in the employee break-room." He shook his head remorsefully. "You're a hard worker, but I'm afraid that you give me no other choice but to let you go."

She nodded in understanding, her face paling.

Ian's head shot up, a wild look in his eyes. "It's not her fault. Don't punish her, punish me. Get a stick. Beat me. Do whatever you have to do."

Finley grinned. The boy was laying it on thick.

"That's enough, Ian," the woman warned.

"It's not fair," Ian argued. He shot Drake a dark look. "You work your butt off at this stinking hotel. Your boss should be thanking you, not firing you."

Drake gurgled, his face going redder than a ripe tomato about to burst. "I beg your pardon."

"That's enough, Ian," the woman said in exasperation.

A single mom. Not married. That was good. Finley looked at her name-tag and couldn't stop a smile from spreading over his lips. "Sunny Day," he mused. "It's certainly original."

Sunny lifted her chin, sparks shooting from her eyes as they met his. "Instead of worrying about my name, maybe you should be more concerned about standing here in nothing but a towel."

He looked down, a rush of embarrassment flooding him. He'd been so taken with Sunny that he forgot about the towel, or rather his lack of a shirt or pants.

Ian sniggered, then placed a hand over his mouth when Sunny gave him a sharp look. He chuckled sheepishly. "Sorry."

"Miss Day, I suggest you pick up your items from your locker and leave the premises," Drake ordered.

"Let's go, Ian," Sunny barked, her eyes shooting daggers. Ian leapt to his feet as Sunny grabbed his hand and pulled him forward.

"Wait," Finley said. He didn't fully understand all that was going down right now—certainly didn't understand how he could feel so invested in a woman he'd only just met, but he knew that he couldn't just let Sunny leave.

Sunny halted, arching an eyebrow, her expression suggesting she was ready to fight.

He looked at Drake. "I appreciate that you're trying to maintain order, but it's not necessary to fire Sunny ... Miss Day," he corrected. "I think you should give her another chance."

Drake's jaw dropped. "But I assumed that under the circumstance—"

"It's all right." Finley smiled to soften the tension in the room. "No real harm was done. Ian didn't actually steal the money." He waved a hand. "Besides, I only have a few dollars in my shorts. Had I known the boy needed it, I would've given it to him."

"He didn't need it," Sunny countered. "Like Mr. Drake said, he shouldn't be running around and making a menace of himself." She shot Ian a frustrated look.

Was she trying to get herself fired? Finley was going out on a ledge here, and he could use a little help. He gave her a questioning look. "Wouldn't it be wise for you to keep your job and give your son another chance?" *Please say yes!* Crazy that he even cared, but there it was—he did.

She let out a long sigh. "I suppose." She gave him a challenging look, and all he could think about was how he could get lost in the depth of her deep chocolate eyes. His gaze took in her lips, perfect for kissing. There it was again ... the strong feeling that they'd met before. "If you think it's wise," she finally said.

He chuckled inwardly. Man, she had moxie. Somehow, she'd turned this thing around to make it seem like she was doing him a favor by staying. "Yes, I think it's wise." He looked at Ian. "Will you promise me and your mom that you'll stay out of trouble?"

"Yes, sir," he said heartily.

"All right." He reached in his short's pocket, pulled out the ten-dollar bill and handed it to Ian. "That should cover plenty of drinks. No need to steal." The spur-of-the-moment gesture was meant to smooth things over. He was surprised to see the displeasure on Sunny's face. "What?"

She snatched the money from Ian and placed it in Finley's hand. A jolt went through him when their skin touched. "You don't reward deviant behavior," she snipped.

Drake looked mortified like he couldn't believe Sunny would have the audacity to act this way to the hotel owner. Truthfully, it was refreshing that Sunny didn't seem to care who he was. Before Drake could collect his voice to speak, Finley piped in, "Thanks for your help, Drake, but I think I can handle it from here. There'll be no more talk of Sunny leaving," he added so there'd be no question.

Drake looked back and forth between him and Sunny. The open confusion on his ruddy face was almost comical. "Um, are you sure?"

"Absolutely," Finley responded firmly. He stole a glance at Sunny to get her reaction, but her expression was guarded. She was holding her cards close.

"All right. Good day," Drake said crisply as he turned on his heel and strode out.

"You didn't have to do that," Sunny said when Drake got out of earshot.

"Do what?" Finley tightened the towel around his waist, wishing that he'd put on his pants instead of worrying about Ian escaping.

"Stand up for me." She jutted out her chin and raked her hair out of her eyes. "I'm perfectly capable of fighting my own battles."

Déjà vu wafted over Finley. Where did he know her from? *Sunny Day*. The name didn't ring a bell. Was *Day* her married name? He searched her face. "How do we know each other?" His pulse increased when he caught the flicker of something in her eyes. Yes, they'd met before. He was sure of it.

"I don't know what you mean," she countered.

He locked eyes with her. "You recognized me when you first came in—called me Fin."

She let out a shaky laugh. "Of course, I recognized you. You own

The Belmont. Your name and picture are all over the orientation material I read when I was first hired."

Was that true? Even as he pondered the question, he knew it wasn't. His name and face weren't on anything. His dad's, maybe, but not his. "I don't believe you."

Her eyes rounded in surprise, her nostrils flared as she tipped her head back. "Are you calling me a liar?"

Wow, it didn't take much to get her riled. He chuckled, a smile easing over his lips. "You know, with a name like Sunny, I would expect you to have a cheerier disposition. Maybe you should've been named Stormy."

Chortles burst from Ian's throat, then he clamped his lips together, both hands going over his mouth to stifle the laughter when he saw Sunny's furious expression. She grunted, eyes narrowing. "That'll be enough from you, Taz," she muttered, shooting him a death glare. "You've caused enough trouble already."

"Taz?" Finley frowned. "I thought his name was Ian."

She made a face. "It is, but I call him Taz for the cartoon character Tasmanian Devil."

"Yes, it fits." Finley chuckled, waving a hand. "Oh, don't be too hard on Ian. Boys will be boys, after all."

Her eyebrow shot up. "You certainly didn't seem to think so earlier when you got Drake to drag me in here."

Finley couldn't remember the last time he'd been this stimulated by a conversation. After the disaster with Emerson, he'd begun to ask himself if he'd ever be attracted to anyone else. A few minutes in the presence of this sharp-tongued beauty and the question was answered with a resounding *Yes!* He couldn't stop a mile-wide grin from spilling over his lips.

Sparks shot from her eyes. "Are you laughing at me?"

"No." He held up his hands in defeat, a laugh rumbling in his throat. "I promise," he added when he realized that she didn't believe him. Ian was looking at him with an expression that said, *You're about to get chewed up and spit out, man.* "First of all, I didn't ask Drake to come in here. He happened to be walking by when he heard me call out to Ian. He took it upon himself to go and get you."

Her eyes softened a smidgen. "Oh," she said, a hint of apology in her tone. She straightened her shoulders. "I'm sorry for any trouble we caused." Her gaze went to the towel, and he caught a flash of amusement in her dark eyes. "I'll leave you to whatever it was you were doing before your day got interrupted. Let's go, Ian," she ordered, grabbing his hand and pulling him forward.

Finley couldn't seem to take his eyes off hers as she strode across the room with the carriage of a queen. His fingers itched to tug on her ponytail holder to release her thick, dark hair so it would tumble freely over her slender, proud shoulders. "Sunny."

She stopped, glancing back. "Yeah?"

It was on the tip of his tongue to ask her on a date, but he suspected she'd turn him down flat. "It's nice to meet you." The space between them shrank as electricity shot through his veins.

She blinked a couple of times. "Thanks."

"I'll see you around." It was more of a question than a statement. He held his breath, awaiting her answer.

"Yeah," she finally said softly, a slight smile touching her lips as she exited the room.

A rush of adrenaline went through Finley. Crazy how quickly things could change. Yeah, he still needed to get caught up on work, but it would have to wait. He hurried into the dressing room to put on his shorts. His next stop would be to Drake's office to find out everything he could about Sunny Day and her son Ian.

CHAPTER 3

Sunny paced back and forth across the living room of her small, rented house.

Of all the hotels, why did she have to pick the one owned by Finley Landers? It was like fate had some vendetta against her. Finley no more believed her flimsy story than a man in the moon. If only she'd stopped to think before she opened her big, fat mouth and called him *Fin*.

Should they pack up and leave this instant? Before Finley found out who she really was? The thoughts of relocating and getting set up in a new place made her chest tighten. It was hard enough to leave her career, her home ... everything and flee into the unknown. She and Ian were just starting to catch their breath. She'd chosen Park City because she had fond memories of coming here once on a ski trip with her dad and Lexi. It was only a few months later they learned their dad had melanoma skin cancer. When he died three years later, it was just Sunny and Lexi. Their mother had abandoned the family when they were kids. Tears gathered in Sunny's eyes as a feeling of complete and utter loneliness overtook her. She still couldn't believe her older sister was dead. She should've known her charmed life as a top designer wouldn't last. Every time something good happened in her life, trouble followed right around the corner. This time, she'd let her guard down, believed that fortune could smile on her, then she got slapped back down to reality. She blinked to stay the emotion, not wanting Ian to see her break down.

It had been a rough two months. Sunny was constantly looking over her shoulder, fearing every minute that Nolan had somehow found them. The one consolation of the entire situation was the familiarity of Park City. As a kid, she was enthralled with the tall mountains, especially in contrast to how flat Texas was. The weather was pleasant this time of the year, as opposed to the relentless Texas heat and humidity.

Ian was stretched over the couch. He looked up from his video game and frowned. "What's wrong?"

Her heart splintered when she saw the haunted expression on his face. The poor guy had been through a lot. She hated that she was forced to leave him alone while she worked. She'd been tempted to enroll him in public school, but didn't have any records for him. "I'm fine," she responded, forcing a smile. Her plan was for them to lay low for a couple of years before she tried to find work in her field. Eventually, she'd enroll Ian in school and would then be able to show proof that she'd homeschooled him.

Due to the abundance of wealth, Park City was an ideal place to set up an interior design business. Sunny didn't want to leave. She'd probably have to find another job though. She sighed heavily, her gut churning. She'd start looking for something else tomorrow. Then again, it had been nearly impossible to find a job that would allow her to bring Ian to work with her. She couldn't afford childcare, and it wasn't safe to leave Ian here in the house while she went to work. She needed the job at the hotel. She'd have to make sure that from now on, Ian stayed out of trouble. And, she needed to avoid crossing paths with Finley Landers. If she could accomplish those two feats, she might just be able to avoid disaster.

She couldn't help but smile a little as she thought of Finley standing before her in nothing but a towel. She'd had a crush on Finley since high school and had kept up with him through social media. In fact, Finley was friends with her on Facebook—or rather, friends with Ashley Reed. She'd not dared to even look at FB since she had to flee, in case Nolan was somehow monitoring it. She could only imagine what her friends must be thinking. Or worse! What her boss Jill thought. It still cut that she'd had to walk away from her career right when it was on the verge of taking off. She wondered who'd been given the job instead of her. Probably Sabrina Lewinsky. A recent college graduate and a junior designer/assistant, Sabrina had been gunning for Sunny's job for the past year and a half since she joined the design firm.

Her thoughts went back to Finley. He looked just as good as she remembered—no, better! A heatwave went through her as she thought about his muscular chest and defined biceps. The boy had turned into a man, a very fine specimen of a man. He had the same playful twinkle in his warm brown eyes which were flecked with gold. His fabulous smile with sparkling white teeth still had the power to send butterflies thrumming in her stomach. How many times had she wished that Finley would pay attention to her? Back then, he'd been Mr. Popular and she was the scrawny geek who sat behind him in English. They'd struck up an unlikely friendship, mostly because Finley needed her help studying for tests. She suspected that he probably didn't even realize that he'd broken her heart.

Finley had been over the moon for Emerson Stein. From what she read, his infatuation carried through to adulthood. They were engaged, then Emerson dumped him for the Titan's quarterback. Was Finley still carrying a torch for Emerson? She made a face. *Probably.* Then again, what did she care? Finley was a blast from her past, certainly not part of her present or future.

Admittedly, it was a little gratifying that Finley noticed her, even when she was wearing her dreadful maid uniform. Had things been different, she would've liked to have gone out on a few dates to see where things went. But knowing that was an impossibility, she'd masked her interest in Finley with open hostility to make sure he got the message loud and clear that she was off limits. The crazy part was, her harshness seemed to have the opposite effect. She still couldn't believe Finley was interested in her. Then again, maybe he flirted with all the girls.

She plopped down on the couch, a swift stab of jealously shooting through her. Finley could have his pick of girls. *The more things change, the more they stay the same.* Emerson Stein must've been crazy to turn Finley down. Sure, the football quarterback she'd married was handsome, but no one could hold a candle to Finley. She reached for the remote and turned on the TV as she surfed aimlessly through channels. Would she run into Finley again?

Despite her best effort to quell them, she couldn't stop tingles of anticipation from circling down her spine. *Heaven help me!* She wanted to see Finley again—was just as enamored with him as she'd ever been. Even the threat of Nolan Webb wasn't enough to keep her from daydreaming about the possibilities.

Sunny looked up as Evie a fellow maid stepped into the bathroom of the room she was cleaning. "Hey."

Evie smiled, chomping on a piece of gum. "Hey, yourself." She glanced at the bathroom, grimacing. "This place is a wreck. Talk about a bunch of pigs."

The waste basket was tipped on its side, half-eaten pizza slices spilled out. Tomato sauce was smeared on the floor, mixed with coffee grains, globs of shampoo, shredded toilet paper, and no telling what else. "My thoughts exactly." Sunny picked up a mound of towels from the floor, walked past Evie, and deposited them in the towel bin hanging from her housekeeping caddy. "What's up?" About her same age, Evie had short, dark hair, several tattoos, and multiple ear piercings. She was the mother of two kids, a boy and a girl, from different dads. Even though Evie looked nothing like Lexi, her free-spirited nature reminded her of Lexi. Sunny's heart hurt as she thought of her older sister. She was still trying to wrap her mind around the fact that Lexi was gone. She swallowed the emotion, taking in a deep breath as she smoothed her uniform. Times like this were the worst, when the grief took her off guard.

"Drake asked me to find you."

Her heart sank. "Is it Ian?" That kid was going to be her undoing. How many times did they have to talk about him staying in the break room?

Evie waved a hand. "No. Ian's minding his p's and q's. I just checked on him."

Sunny put a hand to her chest. "Thank heavens. I appreciate you checking on him."

"No prob." Evie held up a finger like she'd just had a new idea. "You know, you could always drop Ian off at my house. I'm sure he'd love playing with my kiddos."

"I wouldn't want to put you out," Sunny hedged. They'd gone through this same conversation too many times to count.

She chuckled. "Between the kids and the dogs, what's one more? Know what I mean?"

No, she really didn't know what Evie meant. Sunny had no idea how to be a parent, and it was starting to grind at her. Weeks ago, her life had been orderly, predictable. Now it was a big, snarly heap of vipers that she was trying to untangle without getting poisoned in the process. "Thanks. I might do that sometime," she said evasively. While it would be nice to have a place for Ian to go, she wanted to keep him close for now to make sure he was safe. Also, from the way Evie talked, her kids sounded wild. Ian was enough of a handful as it was without adding fuel to the fire.

Evie twirled her hand. "The invitation's always open."

"Thanks. I appreciate that. You said Drake asked you to find me?" she prompted, putting the conversation back on track.

"Oh, yeah. He needs you to restock the towels in the indoor pool area and tidy things up."

"Okay." She wondered why he hadn't just asked Evie. The question must've been written on her face because Evie shrugged.

"I dunno why he wanted you. Who knows what crazy thoughts

are twisting through Drake's bald head." She brought her finger to her ear and made a circular motion. "Cuckoo," she chimed.

Sunny laughed. Drake was a little strange. Nice, but eccentric.

"Anyway, Drake asked me to take over for you." She wrinkled her nose. "From the looks of things, I'd say you're getting the better end of the deal. Pigs," she muttered. "Some people shouldn't be allowed to stay at hotels."

"Amen," Sunny chirped, handing Evie her bottle of cleaning solution as she went out the door. As Sunny walked down the hall and pushed the button to get on the elevator, her thoughts went to Finley. All day long, she'd feared she'd run into him, but hadn't. She should feel relief, but instead was disappointed. She clenched her fist. Why in the heck did she even care? One chance meeting with Finley, and he was consuming her thoughts once more. This time, however, the stakes were much higher. She was no longer a naïve schoolgirl. She knew the risks. Why was she even thinking about Finley Landers? Why was his face the last thing that flashed before her mind when she went to sleep the night before? The thing with Finley had been a silly crush. He barely knew she existed. She was merely the mousy girl who sat in the seat behind him, the non-threatening friend he could confide in, the Brainiac who could help him with his assignments. She grunted. She was being far too generous in her description of herself. If she were a real Brainiac, she could find a way to navigate Ian and the Nolan Webb threat. She shook her head, her thoughts returning to Finley. The fact that she looked familiar to him was miraculous.

She stepped into the pool area, expecting to find it brimming with people. Was it closed for a private gathering? There was probably a sign on the door, but she'd been too consumed with her own thoughts to notice. She heard movement and was surprised to see a lone swimmer. Her heart nearly stopped when she realized it was Finley. He was slicing through the water in neat strokes, his muscles moving like a fine-oiled machine under his tanned skin. Her throat went dry as she swallowed. *Geez.* It was unfair for a man to look that good. How was she supposed to remain unaffected by him? Had

Finley arranged this so he could be alone with her? The notion sent excitement brimming in her chest. She snuffed it out and forced her feet to move forward to the towel closet. Her pulse drumming against her neck, she removed a neat stack of towels and placed them in the open cabinet. Then she commenced picking up the wet towels littered over the cement floor. Finley was at the other end of the pool, seemingly oblivious that she was even here. She glanced at the towels near where he was. She'd have to get those too. Her heart pounding, she went over to get them. Maybe he'd be too focused on swimming to notice her.

One towel, then two. So far so good. He didn't even act as though he knew she was here. *It's for the best*, she told herself, pushing aside the disappointment. *Hurry*, her mind screamed. A few more towels and she'd be done. She picked up the last one and was about to scamper to the bin to deposit them and then dart out.

"Hey."

His voice sent quivers of awareness over her as she slowly turned.

She watched in fascination as he climbed up the ladder with the ease and grace of a gymnast. An unexpected wave of desire simmered in her stomach, sending heat bursting over her. He looked like a freaking Adonis.

Crap, Crap, Crap! Now what?

CHAPTER 4

Sunny fought to keep her face expressionless as her eyes went to Finley's pecs. *Don't stare*, the little voice in her head commanded, but she couldn't seem to peel her eyes away. Water droplets trickled down his skin as he brushed the water from his face, then ran his hands through his hair. She felt like she was watching a live fitness commercial.

"Would you mind handing me a towel?"

She looked down at the damp towels she was holding. Her first impulse was to thrust them at him. Then it registered in her mind that he wanted a fresh towel. "Sure." She hurried to the bin on the other side of the pool and dropped in the towels. Next, she reached for a clean towel and went back to him, keenly aware the entire time that he was watching her. His skin shimmered gold, the proportions of his body perfect. A part of her wondered if maybe this was a dream. Maybe the nightmarish events in her life were too much for her brain to take, so she was dreaming up her greatest fantasy— Finley Landers here in the hotel. Sooner or later, she'd wake up. Amusement sparkled in his compelling eyes, which were more gold than brown today. "The towel?" He arched an eyebrow.

"Oh." Her cheeks flushed as she held it out. Why did she have to act like a complete idiot around him? Finley took it from her, brushing her hand in the process.

"Thanks," he said offhandedly, flashing a dazzling smile that caused her breath to hitch.

Finley towered over her five feet four frame. She loved tall, lithe guys. No, what she loved was Finley. Finley had been her first crush, the one who became the pattern of what she looked for in a guy. For her, he embodied perfection. She looked up at his messy hair, which held water droplets. As he dried off, she stood there awkwardly, trying to think up something halfway intelligent to say, but all thoughts seemed to have escaped her head.

"It's Sunny, isn't it?" Finley said, a grin tugging at his lips.

"Yes." From the way he spoke, it seemed like it took effort to recall her name. Suddenly she felt foolish for working herself into a frenzy. As far as he was concerned, yesterday was merely a casual meeting. She meant no more to him than a passing stranger.

"Sunny Day," he murmured, his eyes caressing hers.

Okay, maybe she meant a little something. A stranger wouldn't look at her with those smoldering eyes. Why had Lexi given her such a stupid name? She had to fight the urge to look upward. If Lexi could see her now, she was sure to get a kick out of the situation.

"What's your son up to today? Ian, wasn't it?" A smile slid over his lips. "Taz."

She laughed, a heatwave running through her. Finley even remembered the nickname. "Ian's supposed to be doing his home-work in the break room. Hopefully, he's staying out of trouble," she said wryly.

His eyes sparkled. "Not rifling through the pants of unsuspecting guests?"

An embarrassed laugh escaped her throat. "I sincerely hope not." She still couldn't believe Ian had tried to steal money from Finley Landers, of all people. She risked another look at Finley's magnificent chest, then realized he'd caught her checking him out. A tiny smirk touched his lips. She straightened her shoulders, eyes narrowing. "Well, if you'll excuse me," she said crisply. "I've got work to do." *Geez.*

She'd have to learn to develop a better poker face. She turned on her heel.

"I wish you'd stay." Sparks raced through her when he touched her hand.

She spun around, a mixture of surprise and attraction warring inside her.

A smile broke over Finley's lips. "We could go for a swim. I reserved the pool for a couple of hours."

A-ha! Just as she suspected! "You set this up." Blast it! She couldn't deny that the idea was thrilling.

His expression went innocent. "Huh?"

She held up a finger. "Don't try to deny it."

He laughed easily. "Okay, guilty as charged. Go swimming with me," he implored, his eyes holding hers.

A giggle rose in her throat. "Seriously?" She felt exactly like she did in high school when she was so enamored with Finley that she could scarcely form a clear thought around him.

"Seriously." He tossed the towel on a nearby chair and stepped up to her.

Her heart hammered against her chest. *Breathe*, she commanded herself. She had to do something to counteract this incredible attraction buzzing through her. Her hand went to her hip, her voice going saccharine sweet. "I don't know if I should be flattered or concerned that the great Finley Landers is giving me the time of day." Yes, that was the best line of defense—to keep throwing him barbs.

His face fell. "Ouch." He motioned with his head. "Shall we sit down?"

"I'll stand, thanks." She folded her arms over her chest. "Why me?"

His expression grew puzzled.

"Why me?" she repeated, pinning him with a steely look.

"What do you mean?"

"You arranged this whole thing, got Drake to ask me to come to the pool area. Why?"

"I'd like to get to know you."

A thrill shot through her. Was this really happening? No! It couldn't happen. She had to remain strong. "That's not possible," she said through tight lips.

He touched her hair, stepping even closer. "Why not?" She felt his warm breath on her face, caught a hint of mint. It was mixed with the smell of chlorine from the pool. A lock of hair fell over his eye, giving him an adventurous, boyish look. Without thinking, she reached up and brushed it back, her fingers lingering on his temple. All she could think about was his nearness. She glanced at his lips, wondering how they would taste.

When his arm encircled her waist, she came to her senses. "What're you doing?" she growled indignantly.

"Kissing you," he said huskily, his eyes going to her lips.

She wanted him to kiss her, wanted it more than she wanted air. The instant before his lips touched hers, she pulled back. "I can't," she muttered. A miserable agony streaked through her. To be this close to Finley and not be able to reciprocate his affection was killing her. She'd have to say something catty enough to put him off. She faked a harsh laugh. "You're not really interested in me. The only reason you're giving me the time of day is because you're bored."

"No, that's not true," he said fiercely.

"Then why're you interested in me? I'm a lowly housekeeper." She looked down at the water pooling on the concrete. "Do you need another towel?" she asked to divert his attention.

He ignored her question. "You're beautiful and kind." His eyes roved over her face as he touched her cheek. Her cells danced jubilantly. How in the heck was she supposed to resist such a man? "And I can tell that you care nothing about my money or influence."

"You've got that right," she snapped, her jaw tightening. Yes, she remembered now. Money and prestige had always been a double-edged sword for Finley. He liked his money, but a part of him wanted to be recognized on his own merit, not for his family name.

His eyes took on a serious light. "I know, I can sense that about you, and you have no idea how attractive that is."

He spoke the words like he was unburdening himself from something deep and brooding. A thought occurred to her. "You say you want to be appreciated for you and not your influence, right?"

"Absolutely."

"And yet you used your authority to drag me down here." She held him with a look, daring him to disagree.

He rocked back, a smile creeping over his lips. "Hah. You set me up. You're good," he said admiringly.

His compliment was more pleasing than she'd dare admit. She arched an eyebrow. "So, why did you use your influence? If you're so opposed to being known by it?"

He looked thoughtful. "Failing to take full advantage of the resources at my disposal would be about as senseless as using a Commodore 64 computer when I've got a dozen MacBook Pros at my side." He smiled like he was immensely proud of the metaphor.

She couldn't help but laugh. Finley had always been into computers. Evidently, not much had changed. "You know, you don't need money to impress women. You could just be yourself."

Hope sparkled in his eyes. "Is that an invitation?"

Her eyes flew open wide. "No, I was talking about you impressing other women."

He grinned. "I knew what you were talking about. And thank you. It means a lot. You really are stunning," he murmured.

She felt a soft puff of his warm breath on her face. His eyes were shining with such sincerity that in another few minutes, she'd be throwing her arms around him and begging him to kiss her. Back in the day, she would've gone to the moon and back for Finley Landers a hundred times over. But he didn't want her then. Now? Irritation pricked over her. Why did it have to be now when she was powerless to do anything about it? "You're so charming," she said flippantly. "Know how to say all the right things to have the women swooning over you."

"I only want the attention of one woman," he said in a low tone. "A dark-eyed, exotic beauty with a keen wit and a sharp tongue."

She put a finger to his lip to shush him. His eyes radiated laughter. "Oh, and she can be a bit bossy at times, but I can handle her."

"Shh! Let me finish."

He nodded.

"If we were anywhere but here, you wouldn't even give me the time of day."

His brows furrowed. "That's not true."

She leaned forward, probing his face. "You sure about that?"

"Of course." A new light came into his eyes. "You speak as if it already happened. We've met before."

Crap. Now she'd done it. "Nope," she said lightly. "Just speaking hypothetically."

He touched her arm, his fingertips trailing like silk over her skin, sending delicious pulses swirling down her spine. "Go swimming with me," he urged.

Everything seemed to slow and all she could think about was Finley. How he looked, how he smelled, the fact that he was in standing in front of her, in the flesh. She was as helpless as a fly caught in a spider's trap. She could tell from the look in his eyes, that he somehow sensed the control he wielded over her. She had to put distance between them—had to keep her wits about her. "Go swimming with yourself," she barked, pushing his chest hard with the flats of her palms. His eyes shot open wide, his arms flailing as he fell backwards. "That'll teach you," she muttered as he sank below the surface into the deep end of the pool. A couple of seconds crawled by. "Okay, you can come up now," she said loudly, her hands going to her hips. The old sink to the bottom of the pool trick wasn't going to work on her.

A couple of minutes passed. Frantic wings of panic fluttered against her ribcage. *Crap!* He wasn't coming up. "Finley." He was at the bottom of the pool, just sitting there. "Come up," she commanded, clutching her throat.

This couldn't be happening!

Yes, it could, her mind answered almost before she could get the thought out. Considering her luck of late, it certainly could. No more tragedies were happening on her watch, not if she could help it! Without another thought, she jumped in to save him.

When she reached him, she reached out to pull him to the surface, but he grabbed her, encircling his arms around her waist as they both rose to the surface.

"What're you doing?" she demanded, slapping his arms. She spat out the water, trying to clear her eyes so she could see.

He laughed and let her go. She moved away from him, treading water. "I can't believe you did that! I thought you were drowning." Her shoes were like concrete on her feet. This whole thing was ridiculous! How was she supposed to go back to work when she was sopping wet? Drake was going to have a coronary over this.

"You jumped in to save me." There was open admiration in his voice. "Thank you."

She just rolled her eyes.

He bridged the distance between them. "Don't be mad. I was just having a little fun," he said playfully.

"At my expense," she muttered, but her anger was ebbing. Dang, these shoes felt heavy. Her dress was billowing up. She pushed it back down, grunting. "I'm sinking," she grumbled.

"Here, I'll hold you up." He slid his arms around her waist.

"I don't need your help," she retorted. It was nice to have his support lifting her up. No way was she going to admit it though. "You've caused me enough trouble as it is. I've got to get out of here before these shoes cause me to sink like a rock."

"Take them off."

"Huh?"

A mischievous smile tugged at his lips. "Take them off, and you'll be free. Just me and you in this big, wonderful pool."

She tried to hold it back, but couldn't stop laughter from gurgling in her throat. A reckless impulse overtook her as she slid off the shoes. Finley took them from her and tossed them over to the side, near the lounge chairs. "I can't believe I'm doing this," she uttered, mostly to herself.

"Cowabunga!" She looked up as Ian sprinted to the edge and jumped into the pool cannonball style, causing a mountain of water to spray over them.

Ian's face bobbed out of the water as he dog paddled toward them. "Hey."

"What're you doing here?" Sunny moved over to the side of the pool and put her arm on the concrete edge. Finley did the same, staying close by her.

"I thought we agreed you were going to stay in the lounge and do your homework," Sunny said, giving Ian a firm look.

"I finished it."

Sunny cocked an eyebrow. "All of it?"

Ian smiled broadly. With his freckles and sparkling blue eyes, he was the epitome of the all-American boy. "Yep." He looked at Finley, his eyes shining. "I did it fast just like you said, so I could go swimming."

She turned and saw Finley's sheepish grin. "You!" she exploded, slapping his arm. She shook her head. "You were acting so sly like you were trying to recall mine and Ian's names. And all the while you had the whole thing planned."

Finley just laughed, not even the slightest hint of remorse in his expression. "My mama didn't raise no dummy," he drawled in an exaggerated Southern accent. He was way to charming for his own good.

"Watch this," Ian said as he dove under and turned a flip.

"Very good," Sunny said when he emerged, giving him a thumb's up.

"There's a ball over there." Ian pointed to the far corner of the pool area. "Can I play with it?"

Finley nodded. "Sure."

In a flurry, Ian swam over to the side and scrambled out of the pool to retrieve it.

Sunny looked sideways at Finley. "You think you're really smart, don't you?" She held onto the side with both hands and dipped her head back in the pool. The water was refreshing. The only thing that would've made the experience better would be to shed the uniform and put on a swimsuit so that she wasn't so constricted.

"I guess that remains to be seen."

"What do you mean?"

He moved closer. "Here's hoping that all of my efforts have persuaded you that I'm truly interested in you." Time seemed to pause as his eyes locked with hers. "Have dinner with me tonight."

It was on the tip of her tongue to shout *yes*. Luckily, her good senses took over before the word could escape her lips. "What about Ian?" She glanced in his direction as she spoke. Ian threw the ball high in the air, then jumped into the pool to retrieve it.

"We'll go to a kid-friendly place."

Finley touched her arm, sending sparks tingling through her. "You have to eat."

"Thanks, but no thanks," she said lightly, disappointment lodging like concrete in her chest. Why did making the right decision seem so wrong? She angled away from him and reached to undo her ponytail holder.

"Here, let me help." Before she could protest, Finley carefully slid the holder down her hair. When her hair was free, he used his fingers to comb through her tresses. There was something intimate about the gesture that sent tingles rushing through her.

"Hey ... mom. Come play ball with me," Ian yelled. He was standing in the shallow end, water at his waist.

Sunny cringed inwardly. The word *mom* always seemed to hang a little on his tongue, like it took effort to force it out. She wondered if Finley had noticed.

"All right," she said quickly. Anything to put space between her and Finley. Before she could escape, Finley touched her arm, his eyes locking with hers.

"I'm not giving up."

The sure promise in his voice reverberated through her with such certainty that it caused a lump to form in her throat. She swallowed it down. "I have to go," she mumbled, moving away from him.

There was a reason people often referred to life as a four-letter word. Everything she'd ever wanted was right here in this pool, hers for the taking. Only she couldn't take it. Not while the threat of Nolan Webb was hanging over her head. If, by some miracle, the threat ever was removed, it would be too late. Finley would be long gone.

She'd never get another chance like this again.

Never.

Tears pressed against her eyes. She pushed back the emotion as she held up her arms to catch the ball. "Over here," she said gruffly the second before Ian tossed the ball.

CHAPTER 5

Finley stood, watching Sunny as she arranged the shampoo bottles on her caddy, then jotted something down on a clipboard. She moved with the grace of a queen. His gaze took in her erect shoulders, slim waist, and toned legs. Even in her gray dress uniform, she was a vision. What was it about this woman that had him tied in knots? Since they'd met, he'd hardly gone a moment without thinking about her. He'd gotten up early this morning so he could get his work out of the way so he could do this. He flexed his hands, taking in a deep breath. *Here goes.* "Hey," he said cheerfully as he stepped up beside her. "What can I do to help?"

She spun around to face him, her eyes saucers. "Excuse me?"

He motioned at the caddy. "I wanna help you clean."

If piñatas had suddenly started falling from the sky, Sunny wouldn't have looked more surprised. She gurgled, her hand going to her neck. "What?" She let out a half laugh and shook her head like she still didn't believe him.

He reached for a cloth. "Put me to work."

Her dark eyes flashed with amusement. "You're serious?"

"Yep. I've thought a lot about what you said. You're right. I need to prove myself to you. Also, I'll get to spend more time with you." He grinned. "It's a win, win situation."

Her eyebrow shot up. "Let me get this straight. You're going to help me clean rooms in your own hotel so you can impress me?" She wrinkled her nose like she could hardly believe what she was saying.

She looked adorable and beautiful at the same time. He stepped closer, pumping his eyebrows. "Will it?"

She shook her head, warm, rich laughter floating from her succulent lips. He could tell she was warming up to him. Heck, he'd clean a thousand hotel rooms if it meant earning her trust. "We'll see," she chimed, reaching for the cloth in his hand as she rolled her eyes. "That's a hand towel, not a cleaning rag."

"Oh." He grinned sheepishly. "See, I have a lot to learn."

Her hand went to her hip as she looked him up and down, a peculiar light coming into her eyes. "All right. You wanna help? I've got something you can do."

"Lay it on me." The energy passing between them was strong enough to light up Manhattan. She had to be feeling it too.

Her eyes lit with some secret joke as she cocked her head. "Hey, I've got the perfect job for you." She reached for something beside her caddy and handed it to him.

He took it automatically, then realized what he was holding. "A plunger?"

"Yep. The toilet needs unstopping. I was just about to do it, but since you volunteered ..." Challenge simmered in her eyes as she gave him a checkmate smile.

He straightened his shoulders, tightening his grip on the handle of the plunger. The gauntlet had been thrown down. "All right. I'll do it."

She chuckled in amusement as she motioned. "Right this way."

A second later, Finley had to fight the urge to gag. The stench permeated the entire bathroom. He averted his face, his stomach roiling. "You really want me to do this?" In his lifetime, he'd faced down numerous cut-throat executives around polished conference room tables, but this disgusting toilet might just be his undoing.

Sunny folded her arms over her chest, eyeing him. "You volunteered."

He coughed. "You sure I can't just take you to Paris? We could be there by nightfall?"

"You're such a baby," she taunted, clucking her tongue. She sighed in disappointment reaching for the plunger. "Give it to me," she said dryly.

His jaw tightened. "Not on your life." He turned to face the toilet with a new resolve. "I hope you know that I wouldn't do this for just anyone."

"Yeah, yeah."

He stuck the plunger in the toilet and moved it up and down. The suction took hold. He felt a mixture of relief and triumph when the toilet drained. He pressed the lever to flush it, giving her a victorious look.

"Here, let me get a bag for the plunger." A second later, she held out a bag as he dropped the plunger in it.

"What else you got on your list?" He wiped his hands on his jeans. Nothing else could be as vile as that. An image of his mother flitted through his mind. She'd freak if she saw him. He laughed inwardly at the thought.

"You wanna clean the shower while I clean the sink and toilet?"

He gave her a cheeky grin. "I thought you'd never ask."

"Let me get you some cleaning supplies."

As he wiped down the shower, he glanced at Sunny. She caught his gaze and smiled into the mirror at him. "You should've seen your face when you saw that stopped-up toilet. I thought you were gonna puke."

He shuddered. "I almost did." That Sunny could do this type of work day in and day out was impressive, and strange. He couldn't help but wonder what had brought her to this point. She was smart. Surely, she had other aspirations. He wondered about her background, how she'd ended up a single mom. There was so much Finley wanted to ask Sunny, but he sensed it was better to keep the conversation light. Let's see, what simple thing could he ask? "What's your favorite type of food?"

She pursed her lips. "Hmm ... aside from chocolate?" A grin split her lips. "I could eat chocolate every meal."

He laughed. "Yes, aside from chocolate."

She pursed her lips. "I dunno. It's hard to say. I like all types of food. Tex-Mex, Indian, Mediterranean, sushi." She squirted the mirror with a liquid solution and wiped it clean with deft movements. "Every once in a while, I like a good old-fashioned cheeseburger, onion rings, and a shake."

"Chocolate or vanilla?"

"Chocolate, of course," she said matter-of-factly. "How about you?"

"Strawberry all the way."

She laughed, the sound filling his chest with warmth.

"I like Tex-Mex too. You haven't lived until you've had Tex-Mex in Texas."

She wiped down the sink. "Really?"

"Yep." He kept his voice casual. "Have you ever been to Texas?"

"Nope," she said quickly. "I'll just get the toilet and then we'll restock the towels and toiletries."

Was it his imagination? Or had she suddenly grown nervous? He got that feeling again, the one that told him that there was more to Sunny than what met the eye. He stood and backed up just as she was rushing past. The two of them collided.

"Sorry," she mumbled.

He touched her arm, peering into her eyes. "No problem," he said softly. The air took on a charge as he leaned closer. "Imagine meeting you here in this small, enclosed space," he joked. His blood ran hotter when he saw the longing in her eyes. An invisible lasso wrapped the two of them together as he leaned down. She lifted her face to his, her lips parting expectantly. He brushed his lips against hers, savoring her taste. Notwithstanding the cleaning rags in his hand and in hers, he slid his arms around her waist and pulled her closer. For one painful second, he thought she might retreat, but then her eyes grew soft. A jolt of adrenaline raced through him when their mouths touched. His lips moved slowly and deliberately against hers. He didn't want to move too fast for fear she'd flee. She was breathtaking, intoxicating. Suddenly, he realized that it wasn't about the place, but the woman. Had they been standing in front of the Eiffel Tower, the moment wouldn't have been more thrilling.

"You'd better get your skinny butt down to the break room on the double," a coarse, unrefined voice said. "Ian's bouncing off the walls."

Sunny went stiff in his arms. Finley looked over to see a short, dark-haired maid with more piercings than a prize pig at the fair. This woman looked exactly how he would picture a maid in a hotel to look and act, as opposed to Sunny who looked anything but.

The maid's eyes bugged. "Oops," she quipped, then laughed. "Maybe I'd better go talk to him, as you're otherwise occupied."

Finley felt sick when he saw the mortified expression on Sunny's face. That feeling intensified when she stepped away from him. "This isn't what it looks like," Finley blurted, then instantly regretted his words. Of course it was what it looked like. They were adults, sharing a kiss. What was the harm in that? "What I meant to say is that kissing Sunny was a privilege."

"Thanks for clarifying that," the dark-haired maid hooted.

Geez. Now he sounded like a moron. The more he said, the deeper the hole he dug. The look of regret on Sunny's face was both confusing and chilling. He could almost read her mind, could tell she was thinking she could never let this happen again. *Why?* That was the million-dollar question.

"Don't worry. Your secret's safe with me, Mr. Landers." She tossed her head at Sunny. "Not for your sake, but for hers."

An awkward silence passed.

"I'd better check on Ian," Sunny muttered.

Finley touched her arm. "I'll do it."

She gave him a questioning look.

"Really," he assured her.

"All right," she relented with a sigh.

He cleared his throat as he nodded to the short-haired woman and pushed past her to get to Ian.

The next day, Sunny went through the motions of work, her mind a thousand miles away. Evie told her she was an idiot for getting involved with the boss. The hard truth was that Evie was one hundred percent correct. It was stupid to get involved with Finley, and him being the owner of the hotel was the least of her worries.

As amazing as the kiss with Finley had been, the after-affects were agonizing. It was like getting a taste of heaven and then having the gates come crashing down, forever barring your re-entry. Sunny kept running through her mind what she'd say to Finley if she saw him, but he was nowhere to be found. Maybe he regretted the kiss as much as she. The thought caused a pit to form in her stomach.

When the last room on her list was clean, Sunny breathed a sigh of relief as she wheeled her cart back to the supply room and clocked out. All had been quiet where Ian was concerned. After yesterday, she'd given him a good tongue-lashing and he promised that he'd chill in the break room. She hated having to keep him there so often. Soon, she'd have to make other arrangements. It was unfair to keep a ten-year-old cooped up in an employee lounge day in and day out.

At least Ian was getting a decent education. The bulk of Ian's schooling was done online with remote instructors. He had several assignments that needed to be turned in today. She was letting him use her laptop. Afterwards, she gave him permission to play a video game. She checked on him during her lunch break, and he seemed to be doing okay. This evening, she planned to take him to a skateboarding park and to get ice cream.

Sunny's heart sank when she walked into a vacant lounge. Was Ian in the restroom? She knocked on the door of the men's room. "Ian? Are you in there?"

No answer.

She tried the handle. It was unlocked. She opened the door and looked in. Empty. Her heart began to pound. Where in the heck was he? Ian knew how important it was to stay out of trouble. She wiped her sweaty palms on her uniform, trying to decide where to look for him first.

"Have you seen Ian?" she asked when Brianna a fellow maid came into the lounge.

Brianna jutted her thumb behind her. "Yeah, he's outside in the bouncy house."

"Bouncy house?" Sunny shook her head. "What're you talking about?"

"There's a bouncy house and a bunch of other activities set up in the courtyard. There's even a food truck."

Crap! Just what she needed—Ian to get in the middle of some-one's party. If Drake saw him, she'd be in hot water. "Thanks, I'd better go check on him." She rushed past Brianna and out of the room. When she got to the courtyard, she paused, looking for Ian. There were a handful of other kids playing in the bouncy house and taking turns going down an inflatable slide. Several couples lingered nearby watching those kids, but it wasn't a huge party with lots of people like she'd assumed. There was a pizza truck and a shaved ice stand. Where was Ian? Off to the right was an inflatable ring with two kids wearing gigantic, puffed-up Sumo Wrestler suits. She was about to glance away, but then something familiar caught her eye. Was one of the kids Ian? She caught sight of his red hair. *Oh, no!* This couldn't be good. What in the heck was she supposed to do with that kid? Her heart did a somersault when she realized Finley was standing beside the boys. He blew on the whistle around his neck and brought his arm down like a referee. The boys went at it, grabbing each other's arms before tumbling to the ground like life-size Weeble wobble toys. When Finley saw her, he flashed a large smile and waved before turning his attention back to the boys. As they got back to their feet, Finley held up Ian's arm. "Blue takes the day," he announced. A trickle of applause came from the three or four adults watching.

She forced her feet to obey her brain's command to move as she walked toward Finley.

"Hey," Ian said exuberantly. "Did you see that?" He held up his arms. "I'm a champion!"

"What's going on here?" She looked at Finley, then back to Ian. "We agreed that you were going to stay in the lounge, remember?"

"I was, but Finley came and asked me to come outside." He waved, his hand encompassing the set-up, his eyes sparkling with wonderment. "He brought all this in for me."

The wind left her lungs as she turned to Finley who had a sheepish grin on his face. Somehow, she managed to find her voice. "You did this?" A laugh rumbled in her throat. It was too much, so kind and thoughtful, yet so over the top. Ridiculous!

He rubbed his neck. "Guilty as charged."

"Why?"

"I thought it would be nice to break up Ian's day a little." He held up a hand, lowering his voice. "I know you don't want me to use my money to impress you, but this wasn't about that. This was about doing something nice for Ian."

She tried to wrap her mind around what he was saying. "So, you put this elaborate set-up together? Most people would've just offered to take him to the park." She didn't want to think about how much this must've cost.

"It wasn't a big deal," Finley countered defensively.

"I—I don't know what to say." She clasped her hands together tightly. Emotion lodged thick in her throat. No one had ever done anything like this for her—err—for someone she loved. Doing it for Ian was the same as doing it for her.

Finley was wearing a white t-shirt, jeans rolled up to his ankles, and Docksider shoes. As usual, his chestnut hair had just the right amount of wave to make it look perfect. She glanced at his cut biceps, remembering how he'd been shirtless at the pool. He looked like a slightly older version of an Abercrombie and Fitch model. Her face flamed when she realized he was watching her watch him. There was a glimmer of amusement in his golden-brown eyes as he smiled.

She spread her hands. "I'm not sure what to think of all this."

"Don't think." He took a step closer, his eyes holding hers. "Just enjoy the rest of the day with me."

Sheesh. Even the timbre of his voice was thrilling. He smelled fabulous—musk and mint combined with a distinct masculine scent. She allowed herself one glance at his lips, remembering how tenderly he'd kissed her. He had no idea how much she'd love to throw caution to the wind and give him a hard, passionate kiss, holding nothing back. She cleared her throat, trying to gain control of her emotions. Her heart was hammering so furiously that if her ribs hadn't been there, it would've pounded right out of her chest. "Finley," she began, "this isn't a good idea." *Be strong*, she commanded herself. *You don't need this right now.*

He brushed a tendril of hair away from her face. "Why not?"

Her breath hitched, her skin sizzling with attraction. She could hardly form a clear thought, much less formulate a sensible argument. "You own the hotel where I work."

"So?"

She let out a long breath. "Must I spell it out for you? It could get dicey—put us both in awkward positions. I mean, helping me clean yesterday was bad enough, but this ..." Surely, he'd understand where she was coming from.

His eyes moved over her face like he was drinking her in. "I'm willing to take the risk," he uttered.

For a second, she was frozen. Time seemed to stop. What she'd felt for Finley before was a crush experienced by a young, naïve girl, but this was something more—something grownup and consuming, like she'd finally come to the end of a long journey and discovered the prize she'd forgotten she always wanted. She stepped back. "Sorry, but I can't." This whole scenario was utterly ridiculous. If only she could just be herself, she'd jump at getting a chance with Finley.

Disappointment flickered over his handsome features as he nodded.

Her heart shriveled. That was that. The end of what might've been. Someday, she'd hopefully look back knowing that she'd made the right decision, but right now, it cut like a thousand knives slicing her insides.

She expected him to walk away but was surprised when he reached for her hand, sending a zing through her. "I'm sure you're starving since you've been working hard all day. You've got to try this pizza. It rivals some I've had in New York."

A halting laugh cracked through her throat, and all she could think about was how her hand felt so protected enclosed in his. "Finley, I just told you, this wasn't going to work." Despite her best effort to shut it out, hope sprang up inside her like a tender shoot in the middle of a barren desert. Was there some way to make it work? Could something good actually happen to her?

"Yes, and I got it, but this is just pizza." A smile played on his lips as a devilish glint lit his eyes. "Unless you'd rather Sumo Wrestle instead. I wouldn't mind getting you on the mat," he said softly. His eyes lingered on her lips. "Maybe steal another kiss."

She could feel her face blaring like a neon sign.

"Which will it be? Wrestling or pizza?"

The challenge in his mesmerizing eyes broke down her last defense. "Okay," she heard herself say. "We'll get pizza." When the warning bells went off in her head, she silenced them. After all, it was just pizza. What harm could there be in that?

CHAPTER 6

Now that the sun was setting, the air had taken on just enough chill to make the fire burning in the pit feel cozy. Finley glanced at Sunny, memorizing the outline of her flawless bone structure. His eye followed the trail of her delicate neckline. She had such an exotic flair with her dark eyes and sable hair that gleamed like polished wood. She felt his gaze and angled to face him, a smile touching her full lips. "What?"

"You're so beautiful," he blurted.

A deep flush brushed her cheekbones as if she'd borrowed a touch of the splendor of the vibrant pink streaks pushing across the evening sky. She looked down, her thick lashes sweeping across her olive skin. Then she tensed slightly, seeming to draw into herself.

Oops. The wrong thing to say. Panic flashed over Finley. Things had been going so well the past few hours, and now he'd ruined it with that one statement.

"Poor Ian's exhausted," she mumbled, rubbing her arms. "I'd better get him home and put him to bed." She glanced through the open double glass doors and into the penthouse where Ian was conked out on the sofa.

Finley touched her arm, the warmth of her skin seeping into his.

"Don't leave." His eyes searched hers. "Please. I didn't mean to make you uncomfortable." Being with Sunny made him feel as though he'd been graced with the presence of a mysterious, beautiful creature. He didn't want to make any sudden movements or missteps for fear of scaring her away.

Her features relaxed a fraction as she nodded. "It's been a wonderful day. Thank you." She let out a low chuckle. "I still can't believe you went to the trouble of renting all of those inflatables."

He gave her a playful nudge. "Admit it. You loved the bouncy house."

An unencumbered laugh escaped her lips. It was warm and rich, floating melodically against the gentle breeze. "It was fun," she admitted.

The three of them—Finley, Sunny, and Ian had jumped manically and rolled around in the balls for a good hour. Then they stuffed themselves with more pizza and mile-high shaved ice. Finley couldn't remember the last time he'd enjoyed himself so much. Afterwards, they came back to his hotel suite where they watched a movie and Ian fell asleep. Even though Finley was quickly growing fond of Ian, it was nice having Sunny to himself.

The mellowness of the evening settled around them as Finley leaned back against the cushion. He was desperate to learn everything he could about Sunny. He suspected from the way she handled herself and the intelligent light in her eyes that she was well educated. He wondered again how she'd ended up as a maid, but didn't want to come right out and ask, for fear of offending her.

"Tell me about yourself," he said casually. He'd learned from Drake that Sunny was from Montana, which was interesting considering her slight Southern accent. Ian had zero trace of a Southern accent, which must mean that he'd grown up in Montana.

She folded her arms over her chest, wariness seeping into her eyes. "What do you want to know?"

Finley's senses went on full alert. Something was off about Sunny. "How long have you been in Park City?" He'd start with the innocuous questions and work his way to the deeper ones.

"A few months."

"Where did you move from?" He caught her slight hesitation.

"Bozeman, Montana."

"Oh, so you're a Montana girl, huh?"

She gave him a fleeting smile. "Yeah."

"The summers there are nice."

She nodded in agreement.

"Last year, it was on a Tuesday," he said with a straight face.

She jerked slightly and then burst out laughing. After the laughter died down, she shook her head. "That was a good one," she said appraisingly.

Her compliment warmed his insides. He stared into the fire rather than at her so she wouldn't feel like he was giving her the third degree. "Did you grow up in Montana?" This was met with silence. He glanced at her, could tell she was trying to decide how to answer.

"No," she finally said. "I grew up in Jacksonville, Florida."

"That explains the Southern accent," he said grinning.

She looked surprised. "You can hear it?"

"Yeah, it's slight, but it's there."

"Yours is thick." A smile played on her lips. "You have that sexy Texas drawl down to a science," she said putting on a thick accent.

He arched an eyebrow. "Oh, so you think I'm sexy? Good to know." It was fun to watch her cheeks go rosy. Before she could get all cagey, he changed the subject. "Wow, your accent's impressive. Very authentic."

She winked. "Aw, shucks, darling, once a Southern girl, always a Southern girl."

"I guess so." A few beats stretched between them. He angled so he could look her full-on in the face. "Tell me about Ian," he implored gently.

Her mouth drew into a taut line. "What do you want to know?"

"How did you end up becoming a single parent?"

She sighed, breaking eye contact with him as she stared into the fire. "I was dating a guy." She shrugged. "I assumed he cared as much about me as I him. When he found out I was pregnant, he wanted nothing to do with me." Regret sounded in her voice. "One day I was living my life like normal. The next, I found myself with a son."

"It must've been hard."

"You have no idea." She shrugged, a small smile curving her lips. "But Ian's a great kid." Her jaw tightened, her voice going resigned. "When responsibility comes your way, the only thing you can do is own up to it." She turned to him. "Unfortunately, life doesn't always work out the way we wish it would," she said wistfully.

The distance between them seemed to shrink. "Sometimes it works out even better than we hope."

She blinked a few times and leaned back like she was trying to put space between them. Disappointment settled like bricks in the pit of Finley's stomach. She was determined to keep him at bay. Maybe it was because she'd been hurt so terribly before that she wouldn't allow herself to trust anyone again. A part of him wondered if he should become invested in Sunny. He certainly didn't want another heartache. Then again, this felt different from what happened with Emerson. Deep down, he always knew that Emerson didn't care about him the same way he did her. He kept telling himself that he could persuade Emerson to change her mind, that his love for her would be strong enough to see them through. That was false thinking. He'd come to learn that love can't be forced. Also, in retrospect, he wondered if he'd truly been in love with Emerson or just fascinated by the idea of her.

"Have you always worked as a maid?"

She let out a self-deprecating laugh. "I know. It's pathetic, right?" Her eyes grew murky as she swallowed like she was trying to hold back emotion.

He touched her arm. "There's no shame in doing an honest day's work, regardless of what that work is."

She nodded, but he could tell that she didn't believe him. Did he believe it? It went against everything Finley had been taught. As the son of a billionaire, he'd been bred to believe that he was a cut above the rest. His dad shouted from the rooftops that a person's value was intrinsically tied to his or her contribution to society. But having spoken that statement out loud, he realized the truth of it. Sunny's value wasn't tied to how much money she made or what she did for a living. All the rich, spoiled, high-society women he knew couldn't hold a candle to Sunny. She was the real deal—a field of fresh, live flowers compared to a truckload of the most sophisticated artificial ones. Sunny was the kind of woman that made him want to be a better man. He suspected that even his mother would be impressed with Sunny. "What did you aspire to become ... before Ian?" He thought it might take her a few minutes to respond and was surprised when her answer came swiftly without the slightest hesitation.

"An interior designer."

He rubbed his jaw. "Impressive. What kind of design do you like?"

"Contemporary, Mid-Century Modern."

Finley knew very little about design, but he liked the self-assured light that came into Sunny's eyes when she spoke of it.

"What do you think of the design of the hotel?"

Her eyes widened. "Huh?"

He waved a hand, encompassing the space. "What do you think of it?"

"It's not bad," she said evasively, her cheeks reddening.

She looked so adorable when she blushed that he almost wanted to keep saying things that would take her off guard. "You're a terrible liar," he countered.

She sat back. "No, I'm not. The design is fine. Albeit traditional and a bit stodgy for my taste, that doesn't mean it's bad. I mean, it was probably great ten years ago when it was first done." She bit her lip, a sheepish expression overtaking her face. "Sorry, I don't mean to be offensive."

"No offense taken." He cocked his head, an idea taking shape. "What would you do to update the hotel? Hypothetically," he added when he saw her concerned expression. The word had the magical effect of smoothing the worry lines from her face as she looked thoughtful, a new light coming into her eyes.

"I'd give it a clean, updated feel—make everything more modern and streamlined. Yet, I'd keep the tones on the warm side to make it feel inviting."

As she talked a-mile-a-minute about the changes she'd make, her face was practically glowing. To never have done design before, she seemed to have a thorough knowledge of it. He loved watching her as she talked with her hands. She was animated, intelligent, enthralling. It was all he could do not to close the distance between them, gather her in his arms, and smother her with kisses. When she'd told him all, she offered a sheepish grin.

"Sorry, I didn't mean to get carried away."

"I loved hearing every word."

"Really?" She gave him a doubtful look.

"Really." He couldn't help it. The temptation was too great. He reached for her hand, electricity jolting through him. He was relieved when she didn't pull away. He closed his hand over hers, carefully like he was holding a piece of precious china. "How would you like to redecorate the hotel?"

Eagerness flickered in her eyes. "Are you serious?"

"Yeah. I can tell you know what you're doing. The hotel needs an update. Even I, the guy who has zero design sense, can see that. You'd be perfect for the job."

Without warning, her eyes clouded. "I don't think so," she said glumly.

He frowned. "Why not? You just said you want to be a designer. I'm giving you the opportunity of a lifetime."

Irritation flashed in her eyes. "That's just it. You're giving it to me." She gave him an accusing look. "Why?"

"What do you mean?" he blustered. *Sheesh.* Couldn't he make one small gesture without her freaking out about it?

She leaned forward, eyes narrowing with suspicion as she jabbed a finger into his chest. "You've only just met me. I'm a simple maid who, to your knowledge, doesn't have an ounce of design training, and yet just like that, you're willing to hand over a huge project to me. I want to know why."

The fire in her ignited something inside him as he caught hold of her wrist and pulled her closer. "Because I see something in you that speaks of greatness. Hearing you talk, I have no doubt that were you given this project, you'd do an outstanding job. Also, since we're speaking plainly, I like you, a lot. You've hijacked my attention, making it hard to concentrate on anything else."

She sucked in a ragged breath.

He reached and fingered a tendril of her hair that had escaped her ponytail holder. Then his hand moved to her cheek.

"We shouldn't," she said softly, but she didn't pull away. In her eyes, he saw the same longing he'd seen the day before. That same longing he felt.

Anticipation raced through his veins as he leaned closer. His lips brushed hers in a small nip that was both teasing and tantalizing. He pulled back, searching her face as he promised himself that he'd only continue the kiss if she wanted him to. Her lips parted in acceptance as his mouth hungrily covered hers. She let out a tiny moan as he threaded his hands around her neck and up through her hair. As his lips explored hers, he did what he'd been wanting to do all day long. He removed the ponytail holder, sending her lustrous hair falling like water over her shoulders.

The kiss sang through his veins as their lips moved in a perfect dance. It was a feeling of exhilaration, and yet it was timeless like the thing he'd been searching for his entire life was now before him. She slid her arms around his shoulders and pulled him closer as if she, too, couldn't get enough. The essence of her wafted over him in sensuous tingles. He caught a whiff of her fruity shampoo, marveled at how delicate, yet strong she was as she responded eagerly to the demands of his lips.

When the kiss was over, he rested his forehead against hers, cupping her cheeks with his hands. "Wow," he uttered, "that was something."

She laughed softly. "Just as good as I'd always dreamed it would be."

He went stiff as he caught the meaning of her words. He pulled back, his brow furrowing. "You know me," he said firmly, his eyes holding hers. "We've met before." He thought he caught a blip of panic in her eyes, but it vanished so suddenly that he couldn't be sure.

A smooth smile stretched over her lips. "What I meant to say is that ever since our kiss yesterday, I've wanted to kiss you again."

For a second, he was puzzled, but the feeling was fast replaced with triumph. "Our kiss was pretty good yesterday, but this was even better just now."

"Yes, indeed," she laughed.

His eyes moved over her exquisite face. "I'm just glad the feeling's mutual," he uttered, his lips taking hers once more.

A few minutes later, Sunny snuggled into the curve of his shoulder. He drew her closer as they turned their attention to the monotonous motion of the orange flames.

"Tell me about you."

The words were spoken so softly that at first, Finley thought he might've imagined them.

"There must've been someone else," Sunny continued.

"Yes," he finally said. "There was." He felt her tense in his arms. A part of him didn't want to open up this conversation, but it was inevitable. She'd told him about her past. Now he needed to do the same.

"What was her name?"

"Emerson." The word drifted up between them and got swept away like a distant memory by the evening air.

"Did you love her?"

"I thought so." He reached for her hand and linked his fingers through hers.

She shifted so she could see his face. "What do you mean?"

He could sense that the next words he spoke would have a strong impact on their relationship moving forward. He wanted Sunny to know who he was, just as he wanted to know everything about her. Maybe it was crazy to feel so attached to a woman he'd only recently met, but there was no denying it was happening. It felt so right to be here with her and Ian. "Emerson and I were childhood friends. I fancied myself in love with her from the time we were teenagers." He paused. "She always claimed that I wasn't really in love with her, but caught up in the idea of being in love. Emerson assured me that when I truly fell in love that I'd understand the difference." He locked eyes with Sunny so she'd get the meaning of his words. He could tell that unnerved her. Time to back-peddle so he wouldn't come on too strong and scare her away. He smiled to ease the tension as he shrugged. "I guess time will tell, huh?"

Sunny grinned in relief. "Yeah." She looked thoughtful. "What happened with Emerson?"

"She fell in love with someone else."

Her face pulled down in sympathy. "Oh, I'm sorry."

"I'm not."

Sunny blinked, hope lighting her eyes. "Really?"

"Really. In retrospect, she did me a huge favor—allowed me the opportunity to find my own life ... my true love. I believe that my feelings for Emerson were preparing me for when I met the right one," he finished quietly.

Sunny cleared her throat, a smile tugging at the corners of her lips. "There's a name for that."

"Really?"

"Yeah, it's called The Romeo Effect."

He laughed. "You mean the Romeo and Juliet Effect? When romantic feelings are intensified due to parental opposition to the relationship?"

She looked impressed. "You know your literature."

"I've had a few classes on the subject."

She shook her head. "The Romeo Effect is something different. Remember how Romeo was first in love with Rosaline?"

"Yes. If my memory serves me right, Romeo was in love with the idea of being in love."

"Yes, and his love for Rosaline prepared him for the real feelings he'd have for Juliette."

A sense of déjà vu wafted over Finley. Again, he got the strong feeling that he'd known Sunny before. A thought struck him. Maybe it was because he'd finally met the right girl. *The Romeo Effect.* It sounded vaguely familiar. Then it came to him like a streak of lightning amidst a dark sky. "Mr. Adair." He felt a sense of satisfaction at having recalled the memory.

Sunny gave him a strange look. "What?"

"I've heard of The Romeo Effect before from my high school English teach, Mr. Adair." He detected a shift in Sunny, wondering what he'd said to upset her. "Are you all right?"

A stilted smile formed over her mouth. "Yep, I'm good."

He searched her face. "Are you sure?"

She laughed lightly. "Yep, I'm great." She snuggled against him, once again facing the fire.

A comfortable silence settled between them.

"What would you like to do tomorrow?" he murmured into her hair. "There's this great sushi place in Manhattan."

She sat up and turned to face him, her eyebrow arched. "And what? We're just supposed to jet over there?" Her expression grew reproving. "Remember? You want me to appreciate you, not your money."

"Yeah, I know." He let out a breath. "I can tell that you already do. So," he continued, "why not put my money to good use?"

She laughed, giving him a tender look. "You're hopeless."

Hopelessly falling for you, he added mentally. "Central Park is gorgeous in the fall. We could take in a Broadway show—one that Ian can watch, of course."

"What about my job?"

"I'll talk to Drake. He can get someone to fill in for you. Besides, if you take over designing the hotel, you won't have time to clean—"

"Wait a minute," she interrupted. "I don't feel comfortable with you just handing me such a substantial project. It's too much."

He rubbed her arm. "The design project is no big deal."

Her eyes bulged. "No big deal? We're talking about a huge renovation costing hundreds of thousands of dollars. That's a big deal," she finished, glaring at him.

Somehow this conversation had taken a wrong turn. The last

thing he wanted was to anger Sunny. "Okay, if you don't want the design project, then fine. No big deal."

Her face fell.

What in the heck was going on with Sunny? "Do you want the project?"

"Yes," she finally said, "I want it, but I know I shouldn't take it." She looked away, sighing.

He reached for her hands, clasping them in his. He brought them to his lips, kissing her fingertips. "Why not?"

"Because you're only giving it to me because we're—" She bit down on her lower lip, her cheeks going rosy.

He leaned closer. "Because we're what?" He couldn't stop a grin from spilling over his lips.

She grunted, rolling her eyes. "Don't play games with me. We're, you know, together."

A thrill shot through him. "What're you saying?"

"Nothing." Her chin jutted out, eyes sparking. "I'm glad you're having so much fun at my expense," she retorted, moving to stand.

He caught her arms. "Hey, don't be mad. I'm just teasing."

"I know," she exclaimed, eyes widening.

"Because I care about you," he countered. "Look, I know this is all new, but it's wonderful. I wanna spend time with you ... see where this goes. Is that too much to ask?"

He could see she was fighting some inner battle. It was frustrating and intriguing. Sunny was a complicated woman with many layers. He touched her cheek. "Would you give us a chance?"

"Yes," she uttered.

The balance had swayed in his direction. "Good," he said, fighting to keep the exultation out of his voice.

Her eyebrow arched. "But we need to take things slow."

"Okay." He chuckled inwardly thinking of the kisses they'd just shared—not exactly taking it slow, but he wasn't about to point that out.

She held up a finger. "And no jetting me to New York for sushi or a walk in Central Park. I need to keep my feet firmly planted on the ground. I have Ian to consider."

"Oh, speaking of Ian, there's this ice cream shop in New York. They have monster-sized sundaes. Ian would love it. We could take him to the toy stores and The Natural Museum of History. And you haven't lived until you've had a hot dog from a street vendor."

She put a finger to his lips. "Slow," she reminded him.

He let out an impatient breath. "Okay, we'll take it slow." *For at least a few days*, he added mentally. Not only did he plan to take Sunny and Ian to New York but also to Paris and Italy. Maybe even to Australia and New Zealand. While Finley had been to all those places more times than he could count, going there with Sunny would make the experience come alive, like he was reborn.

Ian's shriek rent the air.

Sunny leapt to her feet, her eyes filled with panic as she rushed inside. Finley followed close on her heels.

"No, don't hurt him!" Ian cried. "Please." He groaned, tossing on the couch.

It only took Finley a second to realize Ian was still asleep. Ian clutched the fabric of his pants, his body going rigid.

"Don't shoot him!" Muffled sobs broke from his throat. "M—om! Don't die!" Tears spilled over his cheeks, his lower lip quivering.

Chills ran down Finley's spine as he looked at Sunny whose face had gone ashen. This was more than a simple nightmare. Something was wrong here. Terribly wrong.

Sunny sat down on the edge of the couch and touched Ian's arm. "Hey." He jerked. "Ian!" Sunny said, shaking him. "Wake up. You're having a bad dream."

He shook his head, twisting his body back and forth.

"Wake up!" Sunny commanded in a firm but kind voice as she shook him.

Finally, Ian opened his eyes. For an instant, he had a glazed look. Then he seemed to focus on Sunny. Tears welled in his eyes as he threw his arms around her and buried his head in her chest.

Sunny rubbed his back, letting him cry. "It's okay," she said. "It was just a bad dream."

When Ian's tears gave way to muffles and sniffs, Sunny pulled back and smoothed his hair. "It's okay."

The tenderness in her voice struck a chord inside Finley. It was obvious that Sunny dearly loved Ian, but there was more to the story. Finley was sure of it.

"You fell asleep on Finley's couch after the movie," Sunny explained.

Ian looked past Sunny as if just realizing Finley was there. Ian looked embarrassed. "I'm sorry," he stammered.

"No worries," Finley assured him.

"That was some nightmare," Sunny said with a laugh, but her voice had a false cheerfulness. She ruffled Ian's hair. "You've been watching too much TV."

Ian nodded. His face was splotchy and red from crying.

"Let's get you home so you can get some rest," Sunny said, helping Ian to his feet.

"I can drive you," Finley interjected.

"No need," Sunny said quickly. She smiled, but it was stiff and robotic. "Sorry about all this."

He tried to connect eyes with hers so he could discern what was happening, but she looked away. Dread churned in Finley's gut. Whatever was happening wasn't good. He watched as Sunny gathered Ian's things and hustled him to the door. She turned, offering Finley a fleeting smile. "Goodnight. Thanks again for everything." Her voice was polite ... forced.

Everything in Finley wanted to stop her in her tracks and demand that she explain what was happening, but he knew it would be futile. Sunny was determined to guard her secret at all costs. "Goodnight," he said absently as she rushed out the door and closed it behind her.

For a few minutes, Finley stood frozen, trying to process what had just happened. Then he went to the kitchen island and picked up his phone.

A man answered on the first ring.

"Hey, Percy, it's Finley," he said briskly.

"Yes, Mr. Landers. What can I do for you?"

Percy Longstreet was a longtime employee who'd worked for Finley's dad long before Finley was even born. Percy wore many hats —detective work being one of them. "There's something I need your help with. A friend and her son that I need you to check out."

CHAPTER 7

Long after Sunny got Ian to bed, she lay awake staring at the ceiling, trying to decide her best course of action. She'd gotten a taste of heaven before crashing back to earth in a fiery blaze. Kissing Finley had been everything she'd ever hoped it would be and oh, so much more. She touched her lips, still feeling the burn from his mouth on hers. Desire simmered through her, then came tears. For one small moment, she'd let her guard down and allowed herself to believe that it was possible to be with Finley. Who was she kidding? A bitter laugh rose in her throat. Fate would never be that kind to her. She and Ian were on the run from a monster who wouldn't stop until he killed them both. Shivers slithered down her spine. The sense of urgency to get away from Park City and Finley was overwhelming. But with that urgency came a powerful sense of loss that hit her like a punch in the gut.

Tears spilled down her cheeks as she closed her eyes and turned on her side, drawing her legs underneath her. It wouldn't be long until Finley figured out who she really was. She couldn't let that happen. There was a small chance that Finley would keep her secret, maybe even help her. But what if she was wrong? She couldn't risk it. She and Ian had to leave tomorrow. She had no idea where they'd go.

Thoughts of starting over were overwhelming, but she'd have to face it. She offered a silent prayer, pleading for help.

Eventually, she drifted off to a troubled sleep.

The following day dawned cheerful and bright. For a moment, right after she awoke, Sunny felt a burst of optimism at the coming of a new day. A second later, it all came crashing down as she remembered the events of the night before. With a heavy heart, she pushed back the covers and got out of bed. She'd need to get everything packed as quickly as possible so they could leave.

Hysteria pricked her mind. Where would they go? Did it really matter? Maybe they'd just get in the car and drive. Starting over would eat away a large chunk of the money Lexi had sent her, but there was no other alternative. A dull headache pounded across her forehead. She pushed her hair out of her face. The first order of business was to make a stiff cup of coffee so she could think straight. Then, she'd take a hot shower and get dressed. She couldn't fall apart now. She owed it to Lexi to pull it together.

Ian was already up and watching TV when Sunny came into the living room. When he saw her, he jumped up, a large smile on his face. "Yesterday was awesome! Finley said we might be able to ride the ski lift up to the old copper mine." He pressed his hands together like he was praying. "Please," he implored, giving her a puppy-dog look. "We can go after you get off work."

Her heart shattered into a thousand unrecognizable pieces as tears gathered in her eyes. It was obvious that Ian didn't remember his nightmare, or at least he didn't understand the significance of all that had transpired.

"What?" he asked dubiously.

Her head was throbbing, pain shooting through her temples with every beat of her heart. She slumped down on the couch and patted the spot beside her. "We need to talk."

Finley poured himself a cup of coffee and took a long sip. His fingers wrapped around the mug, he walked over to the double glass doors and looked out. Normally, he had a great appreciation for the spectacular view of the manicured golf course and the towering mountains beyond. Today, however, he hardly noticed as his mind was on Sunny. It would most likely be a few days before Percy got back to him about Sunny and Ian's background. He took another drink of coffee, wincing as the hot liquid burned down his throat. He'd hardly gotten a wink of sleep the night before. His mind kept replaying everything that Ian said. *Don't shoot him.* And then, *Mom. Don't die.*

The part that bothered Finley the most was that it sounded like Ian's mom had died. But Sunny was Ian's mom. His mind caught on something—when he caught Ian in the sauna area, Ian said his aunt would kill him if she found out what he'd done. He tightened his hold on the mug. Was Sunny Ian's aunt? Why would Sunny lie about being Ian's mother?

Maybe he was looking at this all wrong. Ian could've been calling out to his mom and begging for someone else not to die, almost as if Sunny had been there too watching the whole thing. Yes, that must be what was happening. That scenario was equally troubling because it meant that both Sunny and Ian had witnessed some traumatic event. Maybe that was why he felt like there was something going on under the surface where she was concerned.

The stricken look on Sunny's face after Ian's nightmare was what concerned Finley the most. She'd hustled Ian out in a flash like she couldn't wait to get away. A chill ran down Finley's spine. Would Sunny just leave? His heart began to pound, and he realized that was the core of his fear. He was worried that Sunny might vanish. The notion was ridiculous—unfounded—and yet he couldn't seem to fight off the feeling of impending doom.

He hurried back to the kitchen and placed his mug on the island. He didn't have the luxury of waiting until Percy got back to him with information on Sunny and Ian. He had to talk to Sunny now. He glanced at the clock—7:20. Sunny didn't start work until 9:00. *It'll be too late then,* his mind screamed. His gut told him that it was imperative that he find Sunny now. He chuckled humorously. That might be hard to do considering he didn't even know where she lived, but he knew someone who did. He picked up his phone and called Drake. *Please answer,* he prayed.

"No!" Ian's face lit up like a sunburn, his lip curling with indignation. "I won't go." He crossed his hands over his chest, glaring at Sunny like everything was her fault.

Panic welled in her chest. What would she do if Ian wouldn't cooperate? "We have no choice."

"What will it hurt if Finley finds out who we are? He's a nice man. Maybe he can even help us."

It was all Sunny could do to keep her voice even as she spoke. "No one can know who we are. If Finley starts asking questions, it could tip Nolan off."

"He won't have to ask questions if you just tell him the truth."

A disbelieving laugh rose in Sunny's throat. "If only it were that easy." Everything was so simplistic where children were concerned. "We don't know how Finley would react if he knew the truth. For all we know, he could go to the police."

"Well, can't the police help us fight Nolan?"

How could she explain to Ian that the police weren't always the good guys? That they could be bought off. "We can't trust anyone." She felt dead and empty inside. "I promised your mom that I'd keep you safe, and that's what I intend to do." She gave him a firm look, leaving no room for argument. "I need you to go and pack your things."

He just looked at her with defiance.

"Ian, please." Her voice cracked, tears pressing against her eyes. "This is hard for me too."

"I like it here."

"So do I."

"I like Finley." He thrust out his lower lip, daring her to contradict him.

"I like him too." A tear escaped the corner of her eye and rolled down her cheek. Hastily, she swiped it with the palm of her hand. "Look, I know this has been hard for you." Several times, she'd tried to talk to Ian about Lexi's death and what incriminating thing he saw about Nolan Webb. But each time she brought it up, she was met with stony silence. Ian was keeping everything bottled up. The only time it came out was in his dreams. Stupid her. She'd been so caught up in her budding romance with Finley that she'd not stopped to think what could happen if Ian started talking in his sleep. "We need to discuss your mom and what you saw about Nolan Webb." She touched his arm, but he jerked it away.

With a shaky hand, she brushed the hair out of her face. Everything was coming at her too fast, in a giant ball of confusion. Her throat closed, and for a second, she couldn't breathe. She willed herself to calm down. *In through the nose, out through the mouth. Take it one step at a time*, she commanded herself. First, they needed to get packed. The next step would be to get everything in the car and drive until they found some place to stop for the night. When they got that far, she'd plan the next step.

"I'm going to start in my bedroom. You will pack your bedroom. Take only the things that will fit in your suitcase." She spoke the words with authority, praying inwardly that he would comply. If Ian didn't, she had no idea what she'd do. She gave him a steely look. "Is that understood?"

"You're not my mom! I hate you!" He jumped up and ran to his room, slamming the door behind him.

Tears spilled over her cheeks as she looked to the ceiling. "Lexi, I don't know where you are, but if you can somehow hear me, please help." Her voice broke. "I don't know how to be a mom." Her pleadings turned to a prayer. "Heavenly Father, please help me. Please keep us safe."

A whisper of peace settled over her, giving her the courage to dry her tears and get to work.

An hour later, Sunny had her suitcases packed. She looked around the bedroom at the mismatched furniture she'd painstakingly scavenged from second-hand stores to make the apartment feel homey. It was surprising how attached she was to these items, even after such a short period of time. She swallowed the lump in her throat as she closed the suitcase and zipped it shut. Hopefully, Ian had made some headway with his suitcase as well. She'd most likely have to help him with the bulk of it.

She went down the hall to his room and stopped at his door, turning the doorknob. It was locked. "Ian," she said as she knocked loudly. "Open the door."

Silence.

"Ian, this is ridiculous. Open up," she commanded, her frustration mounting. She wasn't in the mood to deal with a ten-year-old's temper tantrum. Sure, Ian had been through a lot, but so had she. The only hope they had of getting through this was to work together. While she wasn't his mother, she was his guardian, and he'd have to learn to respect her. "Open the door," she yelled.

Nothing.

Fear lodged thick in her throat. Was he okay? She pounded on the door, fresh tears welling in her eyes. "Ian!"

She rushed into the bathroom and grabbed a bobby pin. She returned a second later, jamming the end of it into the hole in the center of the knob. She worked the lock until the door opened. "You'd better have a good explanation for this," she muttered, charging in. She let out a strangled cry, her hand going over her heart when she saw the open window. The curtain was still moving. She ran over to it. Ian was running across the yard. He was wearing his backpack, his skateboard tucked under his arm. He glanced back over his shoulder.

"Stop!" she yelled. To her dismay, he kept going. When he

reached the road, he put his skateboard down and hopped on. Sunny cursed under her breath as she ran out of the room, her only thought to get to Ian.

―――――――

According to the GPS, Finley was almost to Sunny's house. Thankfully, he'd been able to reach Drake who gave him her address. Just as he feared, Sunny didn't show up for work. His intuition told him that she was running. He glanced around at the middle to lower-class neighborhood. Exactly what he would've expected from a single mother who worked as a maid in a hotel. However, it was obvious that Sunny was well-educated. Her demeanor spoke of class, and she knew a ton about design. She'd used technical terms to describe the changes she would like to make to the hotel. Not only that, but she'd spoken with absolute confidence, which is why he had no reservations about giving her such a huge project. Regardless of what Sunny said, she wasn't a novice.

As he turned onto the street where Sunny lived, he glanced over and saw a kid sitting on the sidewalk, holding his arm, tears streaming down his face. He got a block past the kid when he realized who he was—Ian! He slammed on the brakes and put the Hummer in reverse. He backed up, put the vehicle in park, got out, and rushed to Ian's side.

Ian's arms and knees were bleeding. He was howling in pain. Finley squatted down and touched Ian's shoulder. "Hey, bud. What happened?"

The words came out in short guttural bursts like it was an effort for Ian to get them out. "I fell—off my—skateboard." He squinted his eyes. "It hurts so bad."

It was at that moment that Finley got a good look at Ian's arm. It was streaked with purple and swelling. He suspected it might be broken.

"Okay," he said mostly to himself. "We need to get you to a hospital."

Ian's eyes widened in terror.

"It's okay," Finley said soothingly. "They'll get you patched up in a jiffy." Ian's face was scarlet, his breathing shallow. The trick was to keep him calm until they could get to the emergency room. "I need to call Sunny and let her know what's going on. She'll be worried sick." He was about to pull out his phone when Sunny came trotting up the street. Her face registered shock when she saw Finley. "What're you doing here?"

Before he could answer, she spotted Ian. "What happened?" she cried, rushing to Ian's side.

"I fell," Ian winced.

Finley looked pointedly at his arm. "I'm afraid it might be broken."

Sunny's hand went over her mouth. "Oh, my gosh!"

"It'll be okay," Finley assured her. "I'll take him to the emergency room."

Her eyes rounded. "No! You can't!"

For a second, he thought he hadn't heard her correctly. "Excuse me? Ian needs to see a doctor," he said quietly.

She moved a couple of steps away from Ian. She started shaking her head back and forth. "We can't take him to the emergency room. It's too risky."

Sunny wasn't making any sense. "Ian needs help."

She touched his arm, her eyes filling with some indiscernible emotion. "Please, we can't."

"Why?" He rubbed his neck. "Look at him. He's in pain. If his arm is broken, it'll have to be put in a cast."

Ian was rocking back and forth, crying softly.

Tears rushed to Sunny's eyes. "Can you send for a doctor, privately?"

What in the heck was Sunny mixed up in?

Her eyes pled with his. "Please?"

The desperation on Sunny's face, cut Finley to the core. She was a good person, he could feel that. He glanced at Ian before reaching a decision. Even if he had to move heaven and earth, nothing would keep him from taking care of Sunny and Ian. "Yeah," he said gruffly. "I'll get a doctor. Let's get Ian back to the hotel."

A sob broke from Sunny's throat as her knees gave way. He caught her arm to keep her from falling. "You'd do that for me?" she breathed, disbelief sounding in her voice.

"Yes, for you and Ian."

"Thank you," she stammered. "You have no idea what this means to me."

He searched her face. "Enough to tell me the truth about what's going on?" Arguably, it wasn't the best time to press her about her situation, but Finley was desperate to know the truth, especially since he was now involved.

She clutched her chest, eyes darting to Ian. An exchange passed between them. Sunny turned back to Finley. "Okay," she said flatly, her shoulders sagging.

CHAPTER 8

True to his word, Finley flew in a doctor from Dallas. His family doctor Leo Stratten was in Canada attending his daughter's wedding, so Finley got the intern who was working under Leo to come instead. Even though Dr. Clint Clock had made it to them in record time, the four hours they'd spent waiting seemed like an eternity. The Tylenol Sunny gave Ian had done little to ease his pain. For the past hour, he'd been screaming and talking out of his head. At the rate Ian was going, there would be little to tell Finley about their situation.

"I want my mom," Ian yelled. "Mom, come back." His lip quivered. "Why did you have to die? I hate Nolan Webb," he screamed. "He killed my mom! And he killed the police officer," he wailed.

"Shh," Sunny said, touching Ian's shoulder. "Try to calm down. The doctor's here." She cast a concerned glance at Dr. Clock who was removing the cap and pushing liquid through a syringe. She could only imagine what he must be thinking.

"I was in Nolan's office." Ian's voice choked, his voice going whiny. "I just wanted a piece of candy from the desk."

"It's okay. Try to relax." Sunny looked at Finley for help, but he could only shake his head.

Ian looked straight ahead, his eyes fixed unseeingly into the distance like he was watching an invisible screen. "Nolan and the policeman came in. Nolan got mad when I went in his office, so I hid behind the desk. The policeman and Nolan started yelling." Ian squinted his eyes shut. "It was loud. I put my hands over my ears. The policeman wanted money. Nolan said he'd already paid him too much. Bang!" he screamed, jerking.

Sunny felt like she was on the verge of losing it. Not only was Finley hearing everything, but worse, so was Dr. Clock. Finley seemed to be reading her thoughts. He placed a hand over her arm. "Don't worry," he said quietly, "I'll have a talk with Clint and explain the importance of keeping everything confidential."

The reassuring tone of Finley's voice helped soothe Sunny's nerves. If he'd not shown up when he did today, she didn't know what she would've done. Everything imploded when she came up the street and realized Ian was hurt. She couldn't keep doing this on her own. She needed help. She needed to trust someone ... she needed to trust Finley!

"This is a mild sedative," Dr. Clock explained.

"I don't want it," Ian screamed, trying to move away, but Dr. Clock caught his arm and pushed the needle into his flesh. "Ouch!" Ian screamed.

Sunny pushed the damp hair from Ian's forehead. "It'll be okay," she said soothingly. She felt like she was coming unhinged. *Please let it be okay*, she prayed. She'd give anything to be able to take the pain away from Ian.

"I want Mom," Ian whimpered, looking at Sunny with desperation.

"I know." Tears welled in her eyes. "I know," she repeated. "Your mother loved you with all her heart." Her voice caught. "She'd be here with you if she could."

She felt the comfort of Finley's protective hand on her shoulder, his fingers seeping warmth into her. Tears dribbled over her cheeks. The cat was already out of the bag. No sense in pretending any longer.

Ian leaned back, his head resting against the pillow. A few minutes later, he relaxed, closing his eyes.

A surge of intense relief came over Sunny, followed by a deep weariness.

"The sedative will help Ian rest," Dr. Clock said. He looked from her to Finley. "Can I talk to the two of you in the other room?"

Sunny nodded, feeling numb as they followed the doctor into the sitting area. She and Finley sat down on the sofa with Dr. Clock in the overstuffed chair across from them.

"The arm is broken," Clint began. "We won't know the extent of the break until we get it x-rayed. There's definitely some angulation of the fracture and it's probably about 30% displaced, but of course we need an X ray to get a precise measurement. If the swelling has caused a gap between the ends of the bone there's a greater chance of non-union. Since it's near the joint we need to get the Salter-Harris classification and decide if the growth plate is involved. And of course we need to know that we're only dealing with a simple fracture. A complex break with several pieces could even mean surgery."

Surgery? No, no, they couldn't go there. The faster the doctor's lips moved, the less Sunny understood. Dr. Clock reminded her of one of those know-it-all students who liked to prove they had a large brain by spouting off technical terms.

Finley glanced at her. She gave him a haggard smile as silent information passed between them. He could tell she was barely holding it together. She was so physically and mentally exhausted that she felt like she might collapse on the floor. Finley reached for her hand and linked his fingers through hers. She was so grateful for his support.

"Why don't you try telling us all this in layman's terms?" Finley said in a musing tone that spoke of unquestionable authority.

Dr. Clock's face reddened as he touched his glasses. "Uh, sure." He cleared his throat. Sunny thought she saw him give a condescending eye-roll. "He definitely broke his arm. Just looking at it and feeling around on it doesn't give me enough information about it. I've done as much as I can to make Ian comfortable for the moment. Do you have access to a facility where we can do x-rays?"

Sunny cried inwardly. Of course Ian would need x-rays! In retrospect, they should've just gone to the emergency room as Finley suggested. Ian would've gotten x-rays and had his arm in a cast by now. She'd feared the fake I.D.s wouldn't hold up under scrutiny, which is why she wanted to handle the situation privately. Because she panicked, everything was now a thousand times worse. Had they simply gone to the emergency room, no one would've been the wiser. Now, thanks to her, both Finley and Dr. Clock had heard everything Ian said. She didn't mind Finley overhearing because she'd planned to tell him everything anyway. But Dr. Clock was another story. Ian had called out Nolan Webb's name several times. Nolan was such a prominent individual that most people knew of him. Ice trickled down her spine. How was she supposed to contain this?

"I'll make a few calls," Finley said, "I'm sure we can arrange to have x-ray equipment brought in."

She turned to him. "You've already been so kind and generous. I hate to keep putting you out."

He squeezed her hand. "It's no problem. I want to help. We're in this together." He leaned over and whispered in her ear. "Like Romeo and Juliet."

Like Romeo and Juliet. Except I hope we have a much happier ending. Tears gathered in her eyes as she gave him a partial smile. "Thank you," she squeaked. "You have no idea how much this means to me."

He gave her a reassuring smile before turning his attention back to Dr. Clock. "I trust you will stay on a couple more days so you can set Ian's cast. Also, I'd like for you to monitor him to make sure everything goes smoothly."

"Yes, I can do that."

"Good, you can stay in one of the suites."

Finley paused, giving Dr. Clock a direct look. "The things you heard Ian say ..."

Sunny held her breath, watching Dr. Clock. Color blotched over his cheeks as he rubbed a hand across his forehead and adjusted his glasses.

Could he be trusted?

Dr. Clock crossed his legs, adjusting the crease on his slacks. "Federal HIPAA laws prevent me from disclosing information about patients."

Finley grunted. "That's all well and good, but this goes beyond a doctor and patient relationship. What I'm asking you—man to man —is can you keep this quiet?" He eyed the doctor, waiting for a response.

"No worries. I won't say a thing." Dr. Clock offered a curt smile that didn't quite reach his eyes. "You have my word."

Slight pause. "I appreciate that," Finley finally responded.

The tension in the room grew palatable as Finley locked gazes with Dr. Clock. In that moment, Sunny realized that Finley was indeed a formidable force. He was sizing the intern up, trying to decide if he could trust him. She felt a rush of gratitude that Finley was in her corner. "Finding people that I can count on ... well, it means everything." The words were spoken deliberately, like a sure promise, maybe even a threat.

"I understand," Dr. Clock said quickly.

"Your willingness to drop everything and come here at my request speaks very well of you," Finley continued.

Dr. Clock's features relaxed a fraction as he nodded. "I was glad to do it."

"Rest assured that you'll be well compensated for your efforts ... and for your silence."

Dr. Clock smile seemed more genuine this time. "Thank you, Mr. Landers, it's my pleasure."

After the doctor retired to his own room, Finley turned to Sunny. "It's time for us to talk."

She nodded, sitting down on the sofa. Her cheeks had a hollow cast, her face pale. She looked fragile, like it was taking a supreme effort for her to hold herself together. He touched her hand, which was ice cold. He wanted nothing more than to pull her into his arms and soothe away the tension, but he needed to know the truth. "Tell me what's going on," he prodded.

She took in a deep breath, her eyes meeting his. "For starters, my real name's not Sunny Day."

The breath left his lungs. He knew she was harboring secrets, but it hadn't occurred to him that she might be using a false name. "What's your real name?" he croaked.

Something shifted in her eyes, and he got the crazy feeling that she was hesitant to tell him. He gave her a questioning look, but remained silent to give her space to speak.

"My real name is Ashley Reed."

He rolled the name through his head. It was familiar.

"I'm not from Montana or Florida. I grew up in Dallas."

His eyes widened. "I was right. We do know each other, don't we?" He searched his brain.

She gave him a slight smile. "Yes."

"How do we know each other?"

She chuckled, a hint of accusation in her dark eyes as she pulled her hand away from his. "See, I told you I was forgettable."

Ashley Reed. Ashley Reed. The Romeo Effect. Mr. Adair. Suddenly, it came to him in a flash. He snapped his fingers. "You went to Trinity Academy. We had an English class together. You sat behind me." He tried to merge the memory of her to how she looked now. "We were friends, sort of. You were really skinny with glasses."

She touched her eye. "Contacts."

He let it all sink in. "I thought you acted strange when I brought up Mr. Adair." A thought occurred to him that nearly snatched his breath away. "Is this whole thing some sort of elaborate scheme?"

"What?"

He gave her a hard look. "Is it?"

She barked out a laugh, shooting him an incredulous look. "Are you serious?"

Horror trickled down his spine. "Did my mother send you here to woo me?" It would be just like his mother to trick him into thinking he was falling in love with a simple maid who was a high-society chick in disguise. The sting of betrayal pinged over him. He'd thought Sunny was different.

She gave him an incredulous look. "You know what? The more things change, the more they stay the same. Everything's always about you, isn't it?" She shook her head, disgust heavy in her voice. "Despite what you think, the sun doesn't rise and set by you." Her voice rose, nostrils flaring. "There's a big world out there that has nothing do with the Landers' dynasty." She jumped to her feet. "I should've just taken Ian to the emergency room and saved us all the trouble. This was a mistake."

He jumped up, catching her arm, a swift panic overtaking him. "Wait a minute. You don't mean that." His world had started anew the moment he met Sunny. He couldn't stand the thought of losing her now.

She let out a humorless laugh. "Yes, Finley. That's exactly what I mean." She gave him a withering look as she started pacing back and forth. "I should've listened to that warning voice in my head and never gotten involved with you." Her hands flew into the air. She waved them around as she spoke. "I've put Ian in jeopardy. Now you and the doctor know about Nolan Webb." She put a hand to her forehead, cursing under her breath.

He felt like an idiot! He'd gotten so thrown off by Sunny's admission about who she really was that he'd forgotten to factor in that other important tidbit—Nolan Webb, the shooting. "I'm sorry." He stepped up to her and touched her arm. "Just stop. Please, so we can talk about this."

She halted in her tracks, her eyes throwing daggers.

He blew out a breath. "You're right. I shouldn't have assumed that my mother was behind this."

The muscles in her jaw flinched with tension. "What you shouldn't have assumed was that I was trying to manipulate you."

"I know." He held up his hands in defeat. "I'm sorry."

They stood, glaring at each other.

Her brows bunched. "Would your mother actually go to the trouble of sending someone to 'woo you'?" She made air quotes with her fingers. "That's a little strange." She rolled her eyes.

"Oh, you have no idea," he muttered. "The last time I saw my mother was at the country club. She'd assembled a room full of women—candidates whose intent was to get to know me in a speed-dating setting, so I could pick one."

"What?" Her jaw dropped. "That's insane."

"Yep, my sentiments exactly."

"What did you do?"

"I started by telling my mother there was no way I was going along with her hare-brained scheme." He winced. "Then she started crying, telling me how much she wanted to find someone for me and how much trouble she'd gone through to put the event together." The shocked look on Sunny's face caused him to chuckle. "I know. It's absurd."

"Just a little," she said sarcastically.

"I shouldn't let my mother get away with her antics. She knows how much I hate to see her cry and uses it to her full advantage."

"What happened next?"

"I paid a waiter to cause a diversion, then high-tailed it out of there. I went to Europe and then came here."

"So, you ran away?"

"Well, I wouldn't put it exactly like that. I've been working remotely the whole time, taking care of my responsibilities in the company." He shook his head, realizing the conversation had gotten off track. He cut his eyes at the sofa. "Let's sit down and talk. I wanna hear the full story about who you really are."

She let out a long breath. "All right." She strode over to the sofa and sat down. He followed, making sure to sit close to her. He could tell she was still peeved at him and for a second, wondered if she might scoot away. Thankfully, she didn't.

He tried to compose his thoughts to figure out the best way to navigate this. "Okay, let's start over. Tell me how you came to be here with Ian. You're not his mother, right?"

A long beat stretched between them. "No," she sighed. "I'm not his mother."

Frustration pinged over him. All that stuff she told him about Ian's dad not loving her enough to stay. It was all lies. He wondered if he even knew the woman sitting next to him. His heart lurched. No that wasn't true. He knew Sunny on a deep, personal level. He cared about her so much that it was unfathomable to think of being without her. He touched her hand. "Tell me."

"I'm Ian's aunt. He's my only sister's child. Everything I told you— about Ian's dad leaving. It happened to my sister, not me."

Ian had referred to his aunt that first day in the sauna area, then corrected himself. It all made sense now.

Her eyes looked luminous and large. The pain in them cut him to the quick.

"My sister's name was Lexi." Her voice strangled. "She was killed."

"By Nolan Webb," he uttered, piecing it together as the horror of it swept over him.

"Yes." Tears filled her eyes. "Lexi was a singer. She had her own show in Vegas. About four years ago, she got involved with Nolan Webb." She drew in a shaky breath. He could tell it was hard for her to talk about what happened. "Lexi's death was attributed to an over-dose of heroin, but that's not true. Nolan killed her." Her eyes hardened. "Ian saw Nolan kill someone."

"A police officer," Finley inserted.

She nodded. "I only learned that part when you did. Ian won't talk about it." She hesitated. "It comes out in his dreams."

"Nolan was afraid Ian would talk. He ..." her voice faltered "... he wanted to silence Ian, but Lexi went to plead with him." Tears misted Sunny's eyes. "She thought she could persuade him to leave Ian alone on the condition that Ian remained quiet about what he saw. Lexi assumed her love for Nolan would be enough to save both her and Ian. My sister was a romantic at heart, incredibly naïve." Her eyes clouded. "The last time I went to Vegas and saw my sister, she had bruises on her arms. When I asked about them, she laughed it off. I suspect that Nolan was beating Lexi." Tears gathered in Sunny's eyes. "Deep down, she must've known how things would turn out because she made preparations for me and Ian."

She told him how Lexi put Ian on a plane to Dallas on the spur of the moment and how the envelope with stacks of cash and fake I.D.s arrived, along with a note from Lexi warning her to take Ian and flee. When she was finished, she sighed like it was a relief to get it all out.

Finley's mind was spinning so fast, trying to take it all in, that for a second, he didn't realize that Sunny was waiting for him to respond. He rubbed a hand across his jaw. "Wow. I can't imagine what you've been through, how hard it has been to walk away from your life."

"It was brutal," she said quietly, a shadow passing over her face. She offered a tight smile. "Now you know the full story."

"What made you come here?"

"I came here once on a ski trip with my dad and Lexi." She shrugged. "It felt like a safe place, and I loved the mountains." She paused. "I never expected to run into you."

He chuckled. "We owe it all to Ian for trying to steal money out of my shorts." He thought that might earn him a smile, but she just sat there, a glum expression on her beautiful face.

He touched her arm. "You need to know that I count it as the greatest blessing in my life that we met—or reconnected," he corrected.

She scrunched her brows. "How can you say that? I've put you in a difficult position." Fear turned her eyes to pools of black. "Nolan will eventually find us." Bitterness coated her voice. "He and Lexi were together. She trusted him, and still he killed her." She clasped her hands together in her lap. "He'll think nothing of killing me and Ian." Her eyes widened. "Or you, if you get in his way."

He looked down at her trembling hands. Then, he gathered her hands in his, lifted them to his mouth, and kissed her fingertips. "I'll protect you."

The look on her face suggested that he was naïve. "Thank you, but don't you see? No amount of money is enough to protect us from someone like Nolan Webb. His resources are as vast as yours, and he's ruthless."

Admittedly, the notion of going head-to-head with Nolan Webb gave Finley the willies, but he'd do anything for Sunny. He squared his jaw. "I'll hire around-the-clock protection. We need to go to the police."

"No," she barked, a crazed look coming into her eyes. "We can't tell anyone. We don't know who might be in Nolan's pocket." The fine lines around her eyes and mouth deepened with worry as she searched his face. "Do you think Dr. Clock can be trusted to keep our secret?"

"Sure," Finley replied automatically. Could they trust the doctor? If only Leo hadn't been in Canada at his daughter's wedding. Leo could be trusted implicitly, but Clint Clock was a wild card.

"I'm sure it'll be fine. I'll pay Clint handsomely to keep this to himself."

The doubt oozing from her eyes spilled out and seeped around them, giving rise to sinister shadows. She shuddered. "I'm not so sure."

"Trust me. If there's one thing I know for sure, it's that money speaks volumes." He gave her a comforting smile, trying to push aside his own fears. "It'll be okay. We'll get through this. I promise."

Tears pooled in her eyes. "You have no idea how much it means to hear you say that. Thank you."

With a gentle hand, he brushed away her tears and pulled her into his arms. She snuggled close, and he kissed the top of her head. "The day you stepped back into my life was the day I truly started living," he murmured. No way he was letting her go.

"Me too. I've had a crush on you since high school," she admitted.

It thrilled him to hear her say those words. "Really?"

"Don't let it go to your head."

He chuckled under his breath. "I still can't believe you're Ashley Reed. You were so quiet and timid back then. Always wicked smart though."

"You were the superstar with an ego as big as Texas." He detected a smile in her voice. "Not much has changed in that regard."

"Hey," he protested, linking his fingers through hers. "That's hitting below the belt."

"It's true."

He pursed his lips together. "I guess I deserved that."

"I would've given anything to have caught your eye, but you were so hopelessly in love with Emerson Stein that everyone else paled in comparison."

Sunny wouldn't be happy to learn that the fiasco with Emerson prompted his mom to take such drastic measures to try to find him a woman. Better to keep that to himself. "Yes, I was in love with Emerson." He felt Sunny stiffen. "Or at least the idea of being in love with her," he added quickly.

She grunted in response.

A comfortable silence settled around them. Finley relaxed against the sofa and then sat back up as another memory assaulted him. "Crap!" Suddenly he realized why Sunny kept making remarks about him forgetting about her. He removed his arm from Sunny's shoulders, turning to face her.

She turned to look at him. "What?"

"The Winter Ball." He swallowed. "It was girl's choice. You asked me to go with you."

"Yep, sure did." She laughed dryly. "You have no idea how many weeks it took me to muster up the courage to ask you."

Guilt clutched his stomach like a tight fist. "I agreed to go and then Emerson asked me at the last minute."

"You dumped me like a hot potato, two days before the dance." The accusation in her eyes made him feel like a complete louse.

"Aw, man. I'm so sorry."

"Yes, you were," she said tartly, her eyebrows raising.

He touched her cheek, marveling at the exquisite woman sitting in front of him. She was everything he'd always wanted and more. *Oh, so much more!* "I was a fool. Forgive me?"

She softened, giving him a slight smile. "Well, you did unstop a toilet for me."

He pumped his eyebrows, trying to look cute. "What other guy would do something so magnificent, so noble, so life-changing?"

"So disgusting." She wrinkled her nose, laughing.

He made a face. "Amen to that. The secret's out. Now you know how into you I am. I'm willing to unstop a toilet to prove myself."

She nudged him playfully. "Well, since you put it that way." She pursed her lips. "Hmm. I guess I could give you another chance. If ..." She made a point of looking at his lips.

"If what?" he murmured. His blood quickened when he saw the desire in her eyes. Her breath caught as he traced the outline of her lips. His fingers traced down the line of her slender neck and then to her collarbone, savoring the velvety feel of her skin.

Amusement flickered over her features as she cocked an eyebrow, moving a hair's breadth away. "Do I have to spell it out for you?"

"No ma'am, you certainly do not," he uttered as he cupped her cheeks, his lips taking hers.

CHAPTER 9

As the lights dimmed, a hush of anticipation came over the crowd. "Ladies and gentlemen, please welcome the one, the only, the stunning Lexi Reed!" the announcer boomed.

Sunny, along with the other members of the audience, jumped to her feet clapping wildly as Lexi strode onto the stage, a large, confident smile on her face like she owned the world. Lexi's natural hair color was brunette—the same as Sunny's—but she'd recently gone a rich, fiery red that caught the stage lights and gleamed like burnished copper. Lexi wore a black sequined dress slit high so that it showcased her perfect legs. Sometimes it was hard for Sunny to believe the larger-than-life woman on stage was her older sister. All those years ago when Lexi took a Greyhound bus from Dallas to Vegas, few people expected her to amount to anything. She took a job as a waitress at one of the casinos and auditioned for a few shows. Her fabulous legs caught the attention of a casting director who gave Lexi the opportunity to be a showgirl in a production, even though Lexi didn't have a bit of dancing experience.

Not only was Lexi a fast learner, but also a hard worker. And while she was an adequate dancer, she had the voice of an angel. She worked her way up the Vegas chain in record time, eventually starring in her own show. Looking at her now with her sleek stilettos and hair swept up in a sophisticated twist, one would think she'd always been a star.

Lexi lifted the microphone to her full, red lips. "Thank you for being here tonight," she said in a sultry, seductive tone that was Marilyn Monroe-esque. A sense of awe came over Sunny when Lexi began to sing. She only got a few lines into the song when her voice squeaked like she'd hit an odd note. A dart of confusion went through Sunny. It wasn't like Lexi to fumble her lines. Lexi's stage persona crumbled before Sunny's very eyes, and she saw a flash of terror on her sister's face as she glanced toward the wing.

Sunny's heart clutched when she saw him—tall, slim, custom suit, jet black hair and matching eyes. Very handsome with polished, patrician features. His hands clutched in tight fists, upper lip curled in disdain, eyes as hard as flint.

The stage vanished and Lexi was in a posh hotel room. She was on her knees in front of Nolan, clutching his pant legs, begging him not to hurt Ian. Nolan leaned over and slapped her hard across the face. Her head jerked like a rag doll before snapping back into place. "I love you," she sobbed. Lexi's tattered cries tore through the air as she tried to shield her face from the onslaught. "Please," she cried, but Nolan's wrath knew no limits as he punched her again and again.

Nausea came over Sunny as she heard the sick sound of bones cracking and flesh giving way to the demands of Nolan's knuckles.

This broken woman couldn't be her sister. Lexi was the strong one. She was a star, destined for greatness. Lexi was her champion, the older sister who saw the world through rose-colored glasses. How could Lexi allow herself to be subjected to this monster?

Stop! Oh, please stop! A sob rose in Sunny's chest. It swelled like a balloon until she couldn't breathe. Lexi looked to Sunny for help. Lexi was helpless and broken—her ruined clothes making a pattern of tattered rose petals over the floor.

Rage overtook Sunny's fear. She'd tear Nolan apart limb by limb if she had to. "I'm coming," Sunny cried, but her feet were embedded in concrete. She tried to get more words out, but her throat closed. "Leave her alone," she managed to say.

Nolan turned to face her, a monster sensing new prey. Sunny looked at a nearby table and saw Ian hiding under it. The world stopped as his distraught eyes locked with hers. A muffled cry escaped his lips. In the blink of an eye, Nolan's attention was focused on him.

"I'm here," Sunny screamed. "Take me instead."

Maniacal laughter encircled Sunny like a swarm of bees. "Don't worry," Nolan sneered. "I'll get you both!"

The scene shifted, and she was running.

"I'm not Sunny, I'm Ashley," she said as she shot up in bed.

For a second, Sunny didn't remember where she was. She put a hand over her chest, which was pounding out an erratic beat as she looked wildly around the room. In a flash, it all came rushing back. She was in a bedroom in Finley's penthouse. She lay back against the pillow, raking her hair from her eyes.

The nightmare had felt so real. She could still feel Lexi's presence. A sense of longing flooded over her, bringing tears to her eyes. Oh, how she missed her sister. She was trembling. She took in a breath, willing her body to relax as she closed her eyes. She wondered if there would ever be a time when her life would return to normal, when she wouldn't have to live in constant fear of Nolan Webb.

Ian's whimper from the room next door sent her up and running to get to him. As she stepped through the door, she froze in her tracks, her heart seizing with terror. In her frenzied state of mind, she thought for a second that it was Nolan. No, not Nolan but Dr. Clock. He was clutching the pillow in both hands, looming over Ian.

Her body stiffened in shock as she stared wordlessly, her heart racing. Somehow she managed to find her voice. "What're you doing?" she shrieked.

Dr. Clock jumped as he turned to face her.

She looked at the pillow he was holding. "You shouldn't be in here." Ian was twisting in his bed, clutching the sheets. Another nightmare. She rushed to his side, glaring at the doctor. "Why are you holding a pillow?" she demanded.

He gave her a perplexed look that quickly gave way to a cool annoyance. "I got it to put under Ian's head. Ian tossed it onto the floor." Dr. Clock lifted Ian's head and put the pillow under it. "What did you think I was doing?"

"I saw you," she countered, "the way you were holding the pillow." A shiver ran through her, and it occurred to her that she was here, alone, with this man whom they knew very little about. Her voice sounded brittle and accusatory in her own ears. "You were going to hurt Ian."

Dr. Clock's face paled, then grew rigid. "Ian is my patient," he said crisply. "I have only his best interest at heart." He gave her a withering look. "You are way out of line."

Confusion swept over Sunny. When she first came in, he looked so menacing. She'd felt hostility from him. It had oozed down the walls and across the floor before crawling insidiously up her spine. Or was it the remains of the nightmare spilling over and coloring her perception? She straightened to her full height, refusing to be intimidated. "Why're you here in the middle of the night?"

"Because I asked him to come in and check on Ian," Finley said as he stepped into the room, holding a glass of water. He was wearing shorts and a t-shirt, his hair ruffled like he'd just woken up. He looked from Sunny to the doctor. "What's going on?"

Sunny tried to articulate an explanation, but the words died in her throat.

"I suggest you ask Miss Day," Dr. Clock said, his lips thinning. "She just accused me of trying to hurt Ian."

Finley looked shocked. "Why would you think such a thing?"

Sunny went colder than a corpse. Then her tongue started moving at warp speed as she tried to defend herself. "I heard Ian's cry. Rushed in. The doctor was standing over him with a pillow. I just assumed ..." Her voice dribbled to silence. She felt like a complete idiot.

Finley walked over and handed the glass to Dr. Clock who

reached for a couple of small blue pills on a nearby tray. "These will help calm Ian," he explained, giving Sunny a frigid look.

She could only shake her head. "I'm sorry," she stammered. She felt small and idiotic.

Dr. Clock touched Ian's arm, causing Ian to jump. "Ian, wake up," he said in a controlled, professional tone, devoid of emotion. "You're having a nightmare."

Ian thrashed, shaking his head.

After a few more attempts by the doctor, Ian opened his eyes. His dazed look suggested that he had no idea what was happening. He looked at the faces surrounding him in confusion, his gaze stopping on Sunny.

She forced a smile, going to his side. For a split second, the image from her nightmare flashed through her mind—Ian hiding under the table, the naked fear in his eyes. She glanced down and realized her hands were shaking. "Hey, big guy. You were having a nightmare." She had to hold it together. She bit down on her lower lip, pushing back the emotion.

Ian winced, touching his injured arm, which was in a sling. "It hurts."

"I'll give him something for pain," Dr. Clock said tersely, reaching for another pill. He held out the glass in one hand, the pills in the other. "Drink this."

"I can't swallow those," Ian gulped, going bug-eyed.

"You can do it," Sunny encouraged. Her nerves were frazzled, stupid tears pressing against her eyes. *Stop being a ninny!* she commanded herself. No way would she break down and let the wretched doctor see her cry. She was just so overwhelmed and exhausted. If only she could get a few hours of sleep, things would look better.

Ian's face crumpled as he shrank back into the pillow. "I can't."

Sunny glanced at Doctor Clock who looked like he was on his last ounce of patience. He placed the glass on the tray with a loud plunk and dropped the pills. "It's obvious that I'm not the right fit for the situation," he clipped. "Maybe you should find another doctor."

Panic rose in Sunny's breast, followed by a blinding anger. This time, she couldn't stop tears from misting her eyes. This was her fault. She'd ticked the doctor off, and now he was going to leave them in the lurch.

A furrow appeared between Finley's brow. For a split second, Sunny thought he was going to chew the doctor out, but then he seemed to get control of his emotions. He held up a hand, a friendly smile touching his lips. "Let's not be hasty, Clint. Sunny meant no harm. She's just paranoid."

Sunny stiffened, not believing what she'd just heard. Paranoid? Seriously? She shot Finley a questioning look. He'd better have a good explanation for calling her that!

A silent exchange passed between them. *Bear with me,* his expression seemed to be saying. "This is all just a big misunderstanding," Finley continued in a smooth tone. "It's understandable that Sunny would be hyper vigilant about Ian's safety ... considering the situation. Think about it, Sunny woke up in the middle of the night to Ian's cry. She had no way of knowing that I'd gotten up earlier and realized Ian was having a nightmare." His eyes met hers, and she was struck by the tenderness of his expression. "You were so exhausted that I hated to wake you up. I got Clint instead and asked him if he could give Ian something to help him calm down." He turned to the doctor. "I'm sure Sunny realizes she owes you an apology."

Sunny looked at Dr. Clock. His smug expression sent even more irritation stabbing through her. What she really wanted to do was tell the jerk to jump off a cliff, but Ian needed his help. It would be excruciating to have to start over with another doctor, especially after Finley had gone to the trouble of flying Dr. Clock in. She sighed, forcing a smile. "Finley's right. I'm sorry, I overreacted. I had no right to accuse you of trying to hurt Ian." Her tone rang false in her own ears.

"We're so grateful that you're here," Finley continued.

Ian tugged at Sunny's hand, fear coating his voice. "Why would the doctor hurt me?" he squeaked.

"He wouldn't," Sunny said quickly. She saw the dark look on Dr. Clock's face. "It was a misunderstanding."

Dr. Clock's features relaxed as he nodded curtly.

Ian's lower lip quivered. "My arm hurts."

"The pills will make it feel better," Sunny said.

"No!" Ian protested, shaking his head vigorously from side to side.

Sunny gritted her teeth. She felt empty and tired. "Ian, you need to take them." She hated the battle-of-wills aspect of parenting.

Dr. Clock rubbed his forehead and chuckled scornfully under his breath.

The hair on Sunny's neck rose. She had to bite her tongue to keep from saying something to the pompous doctor that she'd regret.

"I beg your pardon." Finley's head shot up as he glared at the doctor.

Red seeped into Dr. Clock's face as he cleared his throat. "I'll leave you to it. Goodnight," he said briskly as he strode out of the room.

"Jerk!" Sunny muttered.

Finley nodded, his jaw hardening. "If we didn't need his help so desperately, I'd send him packing."

She sighed. "Unfortunately, we do need his help." She went to the tray and picked up the glass and pills, turning her attention back to Ian. It took effort to put a lilt in her voice. "You need to swallow these. It's easy. Put them on your tongue and drink a big drink of water. They'll go right down without you even realizing it." She smiled, hoping it would help put Ian at ease.

No dice. Ian grimaced, averting his face.

"Ian!" she exclaimed in exasperation. "Enough of this!"

She jumped slightly when Finley touched her shoulder. "Let me help." Finley held out his hands for her to give him the glass and pills.

"Sure. Why not?" She handed the items to him, then backed away, letting Finley take her place at Ian's bedside.

"Hey," Finley began conversationally. He motioned with his head. "Your arm's hurting, huh?"

Ian nodded, looking suspicious. "I'm not taking no pills," he muttered, his brows darting together.

"You're being ridiculous," Sunny snapped. "The pills will help you get better." She was bone tired and sick of going rounds with Ian. The kid was exasperating!

Finley glanced back at her over his shoulder. "I've got this," he said quietly.

Her eyebrow arched. *We'll see*, she said mentally, folding her arms over her chest.

"When I was your age, I didn't like taking pills either," Finley said.

"Really?" Ian asked dubiously.

"Really." Finley laughed under his breath. "My mom would get so frustrated because I wouldn't take them. She'd fuss and threaten to tan my hide."

"Like Sunny?" Ian asked sheepishly, glancing around Finley to her.

Finley laughed. "Yes, exactly like Sunny."

"I didn't say anything about tanning your hide," Sunny grunted. "But I should have."

Ian's eyes rounded, worry etching his features. A second later, his face caved, tears pooling in his eyes. "My arm hurts so bad," he whined.

This whole thing was so dang frustrating! Sunny would take the pain on herself if she could. If Dr. Clock hadn't been such a newbie, he would've realized that most ten-year-old kids had a difficult time swallowing pills. Why couldn't he have gotten liquids? If Finley couldn't persuade Ian to take the pills, Sunny planned to grind them up and stir them in pudding. The hotel kitchen was closed for the night, but surely, they'd have some sort of pudding on hand. Otherwise, she'd have to find a grocery store open 24 hours. The mere thought of going out tonight caused her body to ache from exhaustion. She offered up a silent prayer. *Please let Ian be able to swallow the pills.*

"My dad had a different approach," Finley continued. "He'd find out something that I wanted and would give it to me if I swallowed the pills."

Interest lit Ian's eyes, crowding out the pain for a second. "What sort of thing?"

Under normal circumstances, Sunny would've balked at bribery, not wanting Finley to start Ian down that slippery path. But seeing how it was 1:30 in the morning, she was willing to try almost anything.

Finley pursed his lips together, looking thoughtful. "Well, that depends. What do you want?"

"A new skateboard."

"I think we can arrange that," Finley mused.

"And an Xbox," Ian added.

"Don't get greedy," Sunny warned.

"Fine," Ian huffed with a heavy sigh. "Just a skateboard."

"Just a skateboard?" Sunny's eyebrow shot up. "You're lucky you're getting anything."

Finley grinned. "How about this? After we get your arm x-rayed in the morning and put in a cast, we'll go shopping for a skateboard."

Ian nodded. His face was pale and pinched like he was in pain. Even as frustrated as Sunny was at Ian, she loved him fiercely. The poor kid had been through the wringer.

"All right. It's a deal." Finley patted his knee. "As long as you realize that you'll have to wait until your arm heals before you can get back on a skateboard."

"Well, then what's the use of getting one then?" Ian pouted.

Finley shrugged. "You can always get the Xbox tomorrow and a skateboard later, after your arm heals."

"All right." Ian managed a faint smile.

"Deal," Finley said heartily. He held out the pills. "Place these on your tongue."

Sunny held her breath, praying Ian would take them. Ever so slowly, Ian reached for them and placed them in his mouth. Finley put the glass to his lips. "Now take a big gulp and swallow." Ian hesitated, then noisily slurped the water. He swallowed then coughed. He reached for the glass and downed a few more swigs.

"See, you did it," Finley said loudly. He took the glass from Ian and set it on the nightstand.

Ian smiled. "Now I get the Xbox?"

"Yep. Tomorrow, after your cast is set." Finley pulled up the covers and tucked them around Ian. It warmed Sunny's heart to watch his interaction with Ian. Finley leaned over and ruffled Ian's hair. "Goodnight, champ."

"My arm still hurts," Ian complained.

"It'll take a while for the pain medicine to work," Sunny assured him, stepping up and kissing his forehead. "Try and get some rest."

After she and Finley left the bedroom and went into the main sitting area, Sunny turned to Finley. "Thanks so much."

He slid his arms around her and pulled her close. "You're welcome."

She snuggled against the comfort of his chest. "I'm sorry about the doctor," she moaned. "The last thing we needed was to make an enemy out of him."

He rubbed her back. "It's okay. I know you're stressed." He motioned to the couch. "Let's sit down for a few minutes."

"Thanks, but I'm so tired." She suppressed a yawn. "I'd better get some rest."

"You'll be able to hear Ian if he needs you," he added. "We can watch a little TV until you fall asleep."

The prospects of falling asleep in Finley's arms was enticing. "All right."

"I'll get us a blanket."

She sat down. He returned a minute later. They snuggled up together and he flipped on the TV and ran through the channels until he found a movie. "How about this?"

"Sounds good to me." She leaned into the curve of his shoulder and closed her eyes, a contented haze coming over her.

"What made you think the doctor was going to hurt Ian?"

Her eyes popped back open, heat climbing up her neck. She

could only imagine how extreme her reaction to the doctor seemed to Finley. "I had a nightmare about Nolan and my sister." She shuddered. "Then I heard Ian scream. I ran into the room. Dr. Clock was standing over Ian, holding the pillow." Recollections of the event came rushing back as she shivered. "The simplest answer is ... I panicked."

Finley linked his fingers through hers and squeezed her hand. "You don't have to be afraid anymore."

Fresh tears wet her eyes. "Thank you," she breathed. A tear escaped and dribbled down her check. She was too tired to even wipe it away. She sighed, letting the tension flow out of her as she turned her attention to the TV. A few minutes later, she felt herself drift off to sleep.

CHAPTER 10

"I understand," Finley said, gripping the phone tighter. "I'll be there by the end of the day." A feeling of gloom settled over him as he ended the call. He glanced over at the sofa where Sunny was peacefully sleeping. Last night, she'd been pale and drawn, her eyes rimmed with exhaustion. After a good night's sleep, the color had returned to her cheeks. She was so incredibly beautiful with her dark hair spilling over the pillow. He drank in her delicate features, her long lashes resting against her cheeks. They'd slept side-by-side on the sofa all night long. Finley loved the feel of her in his arms.

Never, in a million years, would he have dreamt that when he came to Park City, he'd find the woman he'd been searching for his entire life. He grinned a little thinking of Emerson's promise about how when he truly fell in love that he'd realize the difference between the infatuation he felt for her and the real thing. Yep, she was right on the money. The difference was startling. Maybe it was too soon to categorize what he felt for Sunny as love, but he knew beyond a doubt that he wanted to be with Sunny always.

Everything would be turning out perfect were it not for the threat of Nolan Webb hanging over them. The episode with the doctor the night before was concerning—how quickly Sunny jumped to the conclusion that he was trying to hurt Ian. Then again, it was only natural that Sunny would be suspicious, considering all she'd been through.

Finley wasn't sure what to do about Nolan Webb. Maybe after he heard back from his detective, Percy, he'd have a clearer picture of what they were up against. He might even talk to his dad about it this evening when he returned to Dallas. He'd know how to best handle the situation. No, scratch that thought. Finley didn't want to create a firestorm where Sunny was concerned. Better to deal with this himself.

He let out a long breath. Sunny wasn't going to be happy when she learned that Finley had to leave for Dallas this afternoon, but it would only be for one day. As soon as the meeting was over tomorrow morning, he'd come back. That had been his dad on the phone. One of their top clients was having major problems with the software implementation on his ranches. He was threatening to pull his business. No way could they let that happen. It would set a bad precedent for future business. Finley's dad scheduled an emergency meeting tomorrow morning at 8 a.m. Dallas time with the client. He insisted that Finley be there to ease the man's concerns.

A part of Finley wondered if he should take Sunny and Ian with him. No, they'd be safer here. For all he knew, Nolan could have men combing the Dallas area in search of Sunny and Ian. Here, no one knew them. They could stay in the penthouse. Ian could recoup and Sunny could start on her renovation plans for the hotel.

Finley heard movement. Sunny sat up, rubbing her eyes. She was so darn cute with her hair all over the place. "What time is it?" she yawned.

"Five after nine."

Her eyes rounded as she jumped up. "Oh, no. I didn't mean to sleep so long. Is Ian okay?" She looked like she was about to sprint out of the room and check on him.

He stood and went to her side. "He's fine." He gathered her hands in his. "After the pills got in his system, he slept like a baby. In fact, he's still asleep. I checked on him a few minutes ago."

"Good," she sighed. "Thank you." She bit her lower lip, her eyes going troubled. "I'm sure Drake's wondering where I am—why I didn't show up for work yesterday."

"Don't worry about a thing. I told him what happened with Ian."

She nodded. He could tell her mind was going a mile a minute. "If I could have the rest of this week off, I could start back next week."

"What?" Finley laughed in surprise. "You don't need to worry about cleaning anymore."

Sunny frowned. "Yes, I do. I have an obligation to fulfill, and Ian to take care of."

He looked into her eyes, marveling at how beautiful she was without any makeup. She looked younger, like a little girl. "I told you. You don't need to worry about any of that."

Her eyes narrowed. "Just because we're together doesn't mean that I expect you to support me and Ian."

Sunny's spunk thrilled him ... and frustrated him. "Of course I'm going to take care of you. Money is no object for me."

She rolled her eyes. "Yes, I know, but I need to be self-sufficient."

"All right. I can respect that. You will be. I'm hiring you to renovate the hotel. You can start as soon as you like."

She tilted her head, sizing him up. "No way you'd give me that job if we weren't together."

He loved the sound of that—them being together. A smile tugged at his lips. "You're a kick-butt designer and could renovate this hotel in your sleep." He could tell from the look on her face that he was right on the mark. "If your life hadn't been turned upside down you'd be designing right now." He pinned her with a look. "Am I right?"

"Yes," she admitted, "but still ..."

He touched her lips as she'd done to him. "No argument. I need a designer and you fit the bill."

She broke into a smile. "You're so dang stubborn."

"Uh, huh," he murmured, "like someone else I know." He slid his arms around her waist and leaned in to kiss her.

She made a face, pulling back. "You don't wanna kiss me," she protested, "I have morning breath."

He laughed. "I'll take my chances." His mouth came coaxingly down on hers as he pulled her closer and gave her a slow, deliberate kiss, drinking in her softness. A sigh escaped her throat as she threaded her fingers through his hair and melted into him, deepening the kiss. Fire ignited through his veins as his hands moved up the length of her back and over her shoulders. The need for her was intense, making him wonder how he'd managed to exist so long without her.

When the kiss was over, he pulled back, his hands cupping her jaw. "You are incredible," he murmured, soaking in the depth of emotion in her rich mocha eyes. He dreaded telling her that he had to go to Dallas this afternoon, especially considering the concern over Nolan Webb. Finley made a mental note to call Percy today to see what he'd found out.

An impish smile tipped her lips. "You're not so bad yourself." She rubbed a self-conscious hand over her hair. "I guess I'd better check on Ian and then get cleaned up."

She moved to leave, but he tightened his hold. "What?" she laughed.

"There's something I need to ask you."

"Yeah?" The sudden wariness that came over her face made him feel for her. She'd been through so much. She deserved some happiness in her life, and he'd do everything in his power to ensure that she got it.

He couldn't hold back the smile tugging at his lips. "Should I call you Ashley or Sunny?"

She chuckled in surprise. "Which would you prefer?"

He made a show of surveying her as he pressed his lips together. "Hmm," he drawled. "Would it hurt your feelings if I said Sunny?"

"Not at all."

"Really?"

"Nope. At first, I couldn't believe my sister had given me such a ridiculous name—Sunny Day." She wrinkled her nose. "She said I was too serious and that the name would remind me to take time to enjoy life."

"You? Too serious? No," he said in mock solemnity.

She shoved his shoulder. "Hey." The corners of her mouth pulled down. "I know. I can be a little too goal oriented sometimes."

"You're perfect just as you are."

She flashed an automatic smile of appreciation, then seemed to get caught up in her own thoughts. A shadow passed over her features. "Now, the name reminds me of Lexi. A connection to her." Tears glittered in her eyes as her jaw worked. She took in a breath and smiled. "I think I'll keep Sunny."

He touched a lock of her hair, giving her a tender look. "It suits you." Now was as good of a time as any to tell her he had to leave. The words were on the tip of his tongue, but then he got distracted by her tantalizing lips. He leaned in to claim them once more, but stopped short when he heard a throat being cleared. They both turned, shocked to see the doctor standing in the room. Finley bunched his brows. "How did you get in here?" He could feel the tension radiating off Sunny as she eyed the doctor with suspicion.

"I knocked, but no one answered, so I let myself in," Clint explained. "The x-ray equipment just arrived." He pushed his glasses up higher on his nose and clasped his hands together. "I knew you both would be eager to get Ian looked at as soon as possible."

"Yes, we are," Finley answered.

"I'll go and wake Ian up, so we can get started." Sunny looked down at her oversized t-shirt. "I guess changing clothes will have to wait."

It wasn't until Sunny was halfway out of the room when Finley realized that he'd still not told her about the Dallas trip. He sighed, rubbing his neck. There would be time after Ian was looked after.

CHAPTER 11

It was a relief to have the x-rays done and Ian's cast on. As they'd all expected, there was a fracture at the distal end of his radius, but it was a clean, simple break and the broken ends were already lined up nicely. Healing wouldn't be complicated at all. Dr. Clock put a cast on him using local anesthesia and declared it might take as long as four to six weeks for the fracture to heal and three to four months before Ian could resume his normal activities such as skateboarding.

Shortly after Dr. Clock set Ian's arm, Finley put him on a plane back to Dallas, this time flying commercially. Sunny was glad to see Dr. Clock go. With any luck, that's the last any of them would see of the pompous intern. Finley assured her that he'd have Leo, his regular doctor take care of the follow-up visit with Ian.

"I believe you made a friend for life." Sunny cut her eyes at Ian who was holding the remote control of his new Xbox with this casted arm and punching the button with his other thumb. His tongue was hanging out of the side of his mouth, his face scrunched as he focused all his concentration on the TV screen. "I'm afraid you're spoiling him rotten though." She made a point of looking at the mile-high pile of video games that Finley had purchased to go along with the Xbox. "You're setting the bar high. At this rate, there'll be nowhere to go but down from here on out."

"Nah. It was nothing. I'm just glad Ian has a way to stay entertained."

She made a face. "For now. Although we'll have to think of something productive to keep his mind occupied besides his online school, which is only capable of commanding his attention for a few scant minutes. Otherwise, he'll turn into a pile of mush in front of the TV."

Finley waved a hand. "It's only been a couple of hours. Let him enjoy it for a while."

She rolled her eyes. "If you say so. This is changing the subject, but what should we do for dinner? I could run to the store and pick up some things for spaghetti. Or we could keep it simple and order pizza." This thing with Finley was more amazing than she'd ever dreamt, but it was happening fast. She was still trying to get her footing, figuring out how to navigate it. Finley had insisted that she and Ian stay at his penthouse since he had three bedrooms. That was all well and good for now, but soon, they'd need to talk about the future. They couldn't stay in the hotel forever. Finley would eventually have to go back to his regular life. Ideally, Sunny and Ian could just go with him, but they couldn't so long as the threat of Nolan Webb was present. One idea would be for her and Ian to move back into the rental house. Sunny got the feeling that Finley would balk at that idea. Maybe she'd wait a few days before broaching the topic. Now that they were getting Ian settled, she was eager to get started on plans for the hotel. While she still felt guilty about Finley just handing her the job, she was well qualified to do the project. It would be nice to have a project to focus on, something to take her mind off Nolan Webb.

"What do you think about dinner?" she repeated, then got a good look at Finley. Her eyebrows shot down, worry spilling over her. Finley was fidgeting with his hands, his face lined with apprehension. She touched his arm. "What's wrong?" she asked, bracing for the worst.

Had Finley gotten bad news from Percy, the detective he'd sent to investigate Nolan? Or worse, maybe he was having second thoughts about their relationship. Cold prickles ran through her. *Please don't let it be that.* She took in a breath, pushing aside the negative thoughts. She had to stop doing this to herself. Every time something good happened in her life, she fretted that trouble was just around the corner. Lexi attributed her rationale to their mom deserting them and their dad dying. "You've got to learn to open your heart to trust people," she'd often say. Perhaps that was true. Sunny needed to rewire her thoughts. Finley had done so many kind things for her. Why was she constantly afraid that he'd fail her?

Finley cleared his throat, his eyes meeting hers. "I've got to leave in a few hours to go to Dallas for an emergency meeting."

Her heart sank. She wasn't fast enough to cover up the despondent look on her face.

He reached for her hand. "I'm sorry. It's lousy timing. There's a problem with one of our biggest clients. I've got to meet with him in the morning at eight a.m. to resolve his concerns. The good news is that I can hop a plane and be back here by tomorrow afternoon."

She brightened a little. It wouldn't even be a full twenty-four hours without Finley. "I'm glad it's work related." She made her voice sound light. "For a minute there, I was worried you might be trying to get away from me because my problems are too large to deal with." She forced a chuckle.

He frowned. "No, nothing could be further from the truth." A fierce look came into his eyes, the gold specks shining like a beacon. "You're the greatest thing that's ever happened to me. I wish I didn't have to go to Dallas. I would love nothing more than to stay here with you and Ian."

She smiled, touching his cheek. "I was just teasing you. I get it. Duty calls. Ian and I'll be fine here while you're gone." She glanced at Ian. "He can work his way through the library of video games, and I'll start drawing up plans for the hotel renovation."

Finley sighed draping an arm around her, pulling her into his shoulder. "You're amazing," he murmured into her ear.

She rested her head against him. "So are you." The comfort of his strong, capable arms settled around Sunny like a protective cocoon, which is why she was shocked at the pit that settled in the base of her stomach. She tried to make sense of her feelings. Part of her apprehension was that she didn't want Finley to go to Dallas, not even for a few hours. She wanted him here with her and Ian. She needed Finley here with her! Crazy how much she'd begun to depend on him in such a short period of time. Her reaction was silly. It was just a few hours. He'd be back by tomorrow afternoon.

Her heart began to pound. Something bad was going to happen. She could feel it. Was Finley's plane going to crash? Would Nolan find her? Maybe he'd already found them. Maybe he was nearby, watching and waiting for the opportune time to strike—a time when Finley was out of town.

She swallowed her fears, laughing inwardly at herself. She and Ian were perfectly safe here. If Lexi were alive, she'd tell her to quit waiting for the other shoe to drop. She'd tell Sunny to be happy, to enjoy this blessed time of falling in love with the man of her dreams.

But she couldn't enjoy it, not when disaster was about to happen. She offered a silent prayer, asking for peace and assurance that all would be well. A measure of peace settled over her, but with that peace came some inner knowledge warning her to be super vigilant for the next twenty-four hours.

Her and Ian's safety depended on it.

It was a little after seven p.m. when Sunny heard something. She looked at the door and saw the handle move. She and Ian were in the middle of watching a movie and eating popcorn. Sunny leapt to her feet, her heart racing. It couldn't be Finley. He'd called her right after he landed in Dallas saying he was headed to his parent's house for dinner.

Ian picked up on her fears, his face draining. "Who is it?"

"I'm not sure," she said, trying to remain calm. Sunny balled her fists, her fingernails digging into her palms. She about jumped out of her skin when the door opened. It was stopped from opening fully by the metal guard on the inside.

"Hello?" a female voice called, pushing against the door.

"Who the heck is that?" Ian said, wide-eyed.

"I'm not sure." Sunny looked at the door. "Who is it?" she called. Her pulse thrashed against her temples. Should she have said anything? If it was Nolan or one of his goons, she'd just clued them in that she was here. She glanced around wildly, thinking how they didn't even have an escape plan. The only thing she could do would be to call 911, and then it would be too late.

"Dede," the woman shot back, like she was irritated at having to announce herself.

"Who?" Sunny asked.

"I'm here for Finley. Open the door," the woman insisted.

Relief swept over Sunny. This had nothing to do with her, Ian, or Nolan Webb. "Finley's not here." Dede. She rolled the name through her head, trying to figure out who she was. Finley had never mentioned anyone by that name.

"Who are you?" the woman demanded.

The woman had a Southern accent. She was haughty, aggressive, territorial.

"I asked you a question."

"It's none of your business who I am," Sunny snapped. She straightened to her full height, glaring at the door. Who in the heck did this woman think she was? "Maybe you'd better start by explaining who you are."

"I'm Dede Chambers." She harrumphed. "I don't know who you are or why you're in Finley Landers' room, but I'm going to give you ten seconds to open this door before I get the manager."

Sunny barked out a disbelieving laugh. "Be my guest." She marched to the door and slammed it shut, locking it. She turned, resting her back against the door, her mind spinning. Who was this woman? What business did she have with Finley?

"Who was she?" Ian asked, but Sunny hardly heard him. She went to the kitchen island and grabbed her phone. She called Finley.

The phone rang once, then went to voicemail. "Hey, it's me. Call me as soon as you get this." She ended the call.

Sunny had just sat back down on the sofa beside Ian when there was another knock at the door.

"Sunny, it's Drake. Can you open the door?"

Her chin going hard, Sunny jumped to her feet, strode to the door, and flung it open. "Yes?" she said coolly. Her eyes first went to Drake whose face was beet red like he might combust any minute. Then she looked at the woman standing beside him. She was tall, blonde, and stylishly dressed like she'd just stepped out of a magazine. She had an indignant expression on her beautiful face.

Drake let out a nervous laugh, rubbing his head. "Uh, there seems to be a mix-up."

Sunny folded her arms tightly over her chest, eyeing him as she waited for him to speak.

"Miss Chambers just flew in from Dallas to see Finley." He cleared his throat. "She's under the assumption that he wanted her to meet him here in his penthouse."

Dede's face hardened. "There's no assumption about it. I'm telling you straight out that Finley asked me to meet him here."

Sunny's eyebrows shot up. "Really? That's interesting seeing as how Finley just hopped a plane back to Dallas for a business meeting."

Dede looked Sunny up and down with scathing eyes, as if Sunny were a bug that needed to be smashed. A haughty smile spread over her lips. "Oh, I see what's going on here." She laughed lightly. "You were under the impression that you and Finley ..." She gave Sunny a look of pity, shaking her head. "Finley, Finley, what have you been up to while I've been away?" she mused.

Drake looked back and forth between the two women. "I'm sure this can be cleared up with a phone call to Mr. Landers." He pulled out his cell phone and stepped away from them.

An invisible fist tightened around Sunny's chest as she fought to get a breath. Hot needles pelted her and then she went cold. She clutched her throat. "Are you saying that you and Finley are together?"

Dede raised a sculptured eyebrow, her voice turning to silk. "Let me guess. Finley had to suddenly go away on business, an emergency that only he could handle."

The breath left Sunny's lungs, and she had the feeling that she was suspended above her body, far removed from all that was taking place.

Dede clucked her tongue. "Finley gets himself into situations and doesn't know how to get out, so he makes up excuses." She shrugged. "You have no idea how many times this same scenario has played out before."

Drake stepped up to them, frowning. "I couldn't reach him." He gave Sunny an apologetic look.

Sunny's mind swam as she tried to make sense of what was happening. Dede Chambers was exactly like all those girls she and Ian had gone to high school with at Trinity Academy. They were catty and privileged and expected the world to hand them their every wish on a silver platter simply on the merit of their name. She detested women like Dede Chambers. Sunny was under the impression that Finley liked her because she was down-to-earth and real, the opposite of those types of women. Had Finley been playing her the entire time? He was part of Dede Chamber's world.

No, that couldn't be right. Finley had nothing to gain from their relationship. Everything he'd done for her and Ian had been out of kindness and affection. What she and Finley had was real. She gave Dede a scathing look. "You're lying."

Dede chuckled. "That would be convenient for you, wouldn't it?" She turned to Drake. "Tell her who arranged for me to come here."

He coughed. "You've made your point, Miss Chambers. There's no need to make things worse."

Ice slithered down Sunny's spine, her throat going thick. "What's she talking about? Who arranged for her to come here?"

"Mr. Landers called a few hours ago and said Miss Chambers would be coming." Drake hesitated. "Since you and Finley were together, I assumed that meant Miss Chambers would be staying in another suite. I guess I was mistaken."

Sunny gulped in a breath, feeling like the floor had slipped out from under her.

"I'm sorry," Drake continued, his mouth forming a grim line.

Dede lifted her chin. "I want this woman out of Finley's room." She turned to Drake. "Do you understand?"

Trembles started in Sunny's hands working their way through her body. She felt someone touch her arm, realized Ian was standing beside her.

"What's wrong?" Ian asked, looking at Drake and Dede.

Sunny could only shake her head. She felt hollow and numb. And furious! Was that why her previous call to Finley went to voicemail? Was he ignoring her? Maybe Finley had cared about her and Ian initially, but then the threat of Nolan Webb proved to be too great. Yes, that had to be what was happening here. Finley couldn't think of a way to break it off with her, so he sent this woman here so Sunny would get the message. Well, she'd gotten it. Loud and clear!

"Let's not be hasty," Drake said. He motioned at Ian's arm. "The boy has been through a lot. He just got his cast put on this morning. Miss Chambers, I'll put you in another suite until we can sort this thing out."

"No, that won't do. I demand that they leave this instant," Dede argued.

Drake gave her a firm look. "I'll have the bellhop take your things to another suite. If that doesn't work, you're free to stay at another hotel."

Dede rocked back, going into drama queen mode as she threw up her hands. "I've never been treated so poorly. This is unacceptable," she blustered. "Mr. Landers is not going to be happy when he hears about this."

Drake folded his arms, eyeing her.

Malice flashed in Dede's eyes. "Fine," she huffed. "I'll stay in another room tonight." She held up a manicured finger. "But I expect the situation to be rectified first thing tomorrow morning. You got that?"

"We'll resolve it as soon as we can get in touch with Mr. Landers," Drake said. "Until such time, Sunny and Ian will remain here."

"Thank you," Sunny murmured quietly, looking at Drake. He nodded, a solemn expression on his face. Kudos to Drake for standing up for her when the chips were down. Too bad she couldn't say the same for Finley. Her heart was encased in a thick circle of ice. Hurt pounded through her, crumbling her insides. Then the anger took hold, giving her the torque she needed to push through the emotion. She'd had the feeling earlier that something bad was going to happen. Lexi accused her of ruining her own happiness because she was too busy waiting for the disaster around the corner. Well, there was a reason why Sunny felt this way. It came from years of conditioning. First her mother left, then she lost her father, Lexi, and now Finley. Tears pressed against her eyes as she swallowed them away. No way was she going to let this horrible woman see her cry.

"Goodnight," she squeaked, closing the door and locking it.

A few minutes later, she called Finley. Again, it went to voicemail. She kept her message short and to-the-point. "You won't have to worry about me and Ian anymore." Her voice caught as she swallowed. "I'm relieving you of any responsibility. Don't ever come near me again," she barked as she ended the call, a sob building in her chest.

Ian also started to cry. "What's wrong?"

She gathered him in her arms and sobbed.

CHAPTER 12

Finley cut off a section of ribeye and placed it in his mouth. The meat was tender, seasoned to perfection. No one could prepare a steak like Louise, his parents' personal chef. He looked across the table at his mom and dad. He'd not realized how much he missed them until just now. He glanced around at the spacious dining room. It had always felt cold and hollow to him. Finley would've preferred to have eaten at the table in the kitchen, but his mom insisted on having a special dinner for him in here.

"How long are you planning on staying?" Fiona asked, taking a sip of wine.

"Just long enough to go to the meeting."

Finley braced himself, waiting for her to put him on a guilt trip for being away so long, but she smiled coyly instead. "I'll be interested in hearing how things go in Park City."

"What do you mean?" he asked carefully. His mother didn't know anything about Sunny, did she?

She waved a hand. "You'll see," she said evasively, her smile growing larger.

He looked to his dad for an explanation, but Kenton only

shrugged. "How was Europe?" He took a large bite of his baked potato.

"Great. Germany was my favorite." As the conversation turned to Europe and his parents chimed in on their favorite places and foods, Finley's thoughts went back to Sunny. He was itching to tell his parents about her, but that wouldn't be wise—not until he could figure out what to do about Nolan Webb. He'd called Percy a couple of times, but it went to voicemail. As soon as Sam returned with a charger, he'd try Percy again and Sunny to see how she was doing.

He forgot to pack his charger and his phone had gone dead. Thankfully, his limousine driver offered to run to the store and pick one up for him. Sam should be returning any minute.

"Did you get the list of Herschel Tolman's concerns for the meeting tomorrow?" Kenton asked.

"Yes, I went over them on the plane."

"What's your take? Can the problems be solved?"

Finley chewed his broccoli and swallowed before answering. "From what I can tell, most of what Herschel's experiencing is user error. We may need to assign one of our guys to cover just Herschel's ranches. That way, they'll have a go-to person to help train and assist on a daily basis."

"Good idea."

Fiona placed a hand on Kenton's arm. "You know my rule. No more business talk at the dinner table," she warned.

Kenton gave her a placating smile. "You're right, darling. There'll be plenty of time to discuss all of this in the morning."

"Are you sleeping in the guesthouse tonight?" Fiona asked.

"No, I thought I'd go back to my place. It feels like I haven't been back there in forever."

"Indeed," Fiona agreed, accusation ringing in her tone.

Finley smiled picturing his mom's reaction when she learned that he'd fallen for an amazing woman who felt the same way about him. Sunny possessed all the qualities that were on his mom's checklist. She was smart, beautiful, accomplished, well-educated, worked for a prestigious design firm. The only thing Sunny wasn't was high society, more reason for Finley to adore her. Surely his mom would see what a great person Sunny was. Well, even if she didn't, Finley was forging ahead. Nothing was going to keep him away from Sunny. He was growing fond of Ian too. Finley's mom always carried on about how she wanted grandchildren. Ian would fit well into the family. He chuckled inwardly. Who was he kidding? His mom would blow her cork when she realized that Ian was part of the deal, but she'd learn to live with it.

Sam stepped into the dining room. "Sorry to interrupt."

Finley scooted back his chair and stood. "No worries. I appreciate you getting the charger for me. Thanks, man," he added when Sam placed it in his hand. "I owe you one." He ripped open the package, fished his phone out of his pocket, and went to the nearest plug.

Fiona sighed. "Is that really necessary?"

"Sorry, I'm expecting some important calls."

Sam shifted, looking hesitantly at Fiona, then back to Finley. "Uh, do you still need a ride back to your place?"

"That would be great." Finley looked at his half-eaten plate of food and then at his mom's frustrated expression. "Do you mind waiting a few minutes?"

"Not at all," Sam said.

"You should go back to the kitchen. I'm sure Louise will make you a plate," Finley offered.

"Thanks." Sam nodded to Kenton and Fiona. "Have a great evening," he said as he left the room.

"What calls are you expecting?" Fiona asked when he sat back down.

"Mainly work stuff," Finley answered, then changed the subject. "Hey, Dad. How's the restoration on your Camaro coming?" Most people would be surprised to learn that Kenton Landers, the business tycoon who lived in a suit in public, was a big car buff. Not only that, but Kenton enjoyed doing the work himself. He and Finley had restored several cars together over the years.

"Really well. I ordered a new stereo that should be arriving in the next couple of days."

"Did you get the electrical sorted out?" There was a short in the system that caused the previous radio to cut out.

"Yep, after much trial and error. The wiring harness was fried. I had to replace it."

"What color did you decide to have it painted?"

"Candy-apple red." Kenton's eyes sparkled underneath his glasses as he slid his arm around Fiona's shoulders. "I'm hoping when everything's finished, I can persuade this little lady to take a ride with me down to the coast."

Fiona laughed. "I'm sure you'll find a way." She gave Kenton an adoring look.

Finley had always been grateful that his parents were close. That's what he'd always hoped to find—a soulmate. He grinned, thinking of Sunny. She'd looked so darn cute in her t-shirt and shorts this morning, her hair a mess, not a stitch of makeup on. He wondered what she and Ian were doing this very minute. The longing to talk to her was nearly overwhelming.

"What're you smiling about?" Fiona asked playfully.

Finley picked up his fork. "Just thinking that I'd better eat this delicious food before it gets cold. It's not every day a man gets to eat Louise's cooking."

"Uh, huh," she drawled, the look on her face making it crystal clear that she knew he wasn't telling her everything.

As soon as Finley got into the limousine headed back to his house, he called Sunny. He swallowed his disappointment when she didn't answer. Next, he checked his voicemail. Sunny's first message asked him to call her. Her voice was off—strained. His pulse increased. Was everything okay? When he checked the next message from her, his blood ran cold. He swallowed hard, a clammy sweat breaking over his brow. How could she just dismiss him from her life like that? Everything had been fine this morning. Sunny had sounded normal when he talked to her just after he landed in Dallas. What had changed between now and then?

He tried calling her again. No answer. "I'm not sure what's going on," he said when he got her voicemail. "Call me back." He tightened his hold on his phone with one hand and rubbed his sweaty palm against his jeans. None of this was making sense. He tried Sunny a few more times. When she didn't answer, he called the hotel.

"This is Finley Landers," he said tersely when the lady at the front desk answered. "I need to speak to Drake."

"I'm sorry, Mr. Landers, but Drake has already left for the day. May I take a message for him?"

"No," he clipped. "I'll try him on his cell." He thought of another idea. "Can you put me through to the penthouse suite?"

"Sure. Which one? The one where Miss Day's staying or the one Miss Chambers is in?"

"Well, obviously the one where Miss Day is staying," he fired back. Why would the girl ask if he wanted to speak to someone else?

"Sure thing," she said quickly, transferring him. The line rang several times, but no one answered. He ended the call and dialed Drake's number.

Drake answered on the first ring. "Mr. Landers, I've been trying to reach you," he said breathlessly.

"What's going on?"

"I wasn't sure what do about your lady friend, so I put her in the other penthouse."

Finley's gut tightened. "What're you talking about?"

"The lady you called me about, Dede Chambers, arrived at the hotel today looking for you. She and Sunny had words."

"What?" Finley coughed, getting choked on his saliva. "Are you referring to Dede Chambers, the blonde from Dallas?"

"Of course. Evidently, Miss Chambers wasn't expecting to find Sunny in your penthouse." He paused. "Or vice versa. Forgive me for saying so, sir. But it caused a sticky situation."

Something Drake said registered. "Wait a minute. Did you say I called you about Dede Chambers?"

"Yes."

Finley's mind scrambled to keep up. "I never called you about Dede."

Drake cleared his throat. "Begging your pardon, but you called earlier today and said Dede Chambers would be staying a few days."

Fire cut through Finley's head making him feel like it would split in two. "No, I did not," he yelled. Sam glanced back at him in the rearview mirror, but Finley ignored him. "Why are you saying this?"

"Someone called today identifying himself as Mr. Landers. I just assumed it was you."

Finley balled his fist, swearing under his breath. "No wonder Sunny left me that message," he muttered. "She thinks I'm throwing her under the bus. That I'm a lousy cheat."

"I'm sorry? I didn't catch that," Drake said.

Who had called, pretending to be him? And why would Dede presume she could show up unannounced? She'd left him a few messages while he was in Europe, but he hadn't returned any of her calls. The answer came to him like a punch in the gut as an image of his mom flashed through his mind. She'd given him that coy smile and made evasive remarks. His mom was behind this. He was sure of it! He rubbed his hand across his forehead, trying to think. "I need you to talk to Sunny, tell her this is all a big mistake."

"Sure, I'll be glad to do that ... first thing in the morning."

"No," Finley exploded. "I need you to go now."

Long pause. "Mr. Landers, I'm not trying to tell you how to run your affairs, but Sunny was very upset about all of this. It's probably best if you give her some time to cool off. I'll be at the hotel by six a.m. and will go to her room first thing. You have my word."

Finley let out a long breath. "All right. We'll go with that. Thanks." He was about to end the call when he realized Drake was still talking.

"Mr. Landers?"

"Yes?"

"For what it's worth. I'm glad this is all a big misunderstanding." He cleared his throat. "Sunny's a good person. I'm glad you're doing right by her."

"Of course. Goodnight, Drake."

"Goodnight, sir."

Next, Finley called his mom.

"Hey, honey," Fiona said. "Did you forget something?"

Finley's blood was pumping like lightning through his veins sending his mind spinning like a planet kicked out of its orbit. He clenched his fist wanting to punch something. "Did you send Dede Chambers to the hotel in Park City?"

She let out a shaky laugh. "What do you mean?"

The innocence in her voice sent his anger rising to new heights. "Mom! Tell me the truth!"

Silence.

"Mom!" he barked.

"Yes, I thought it would be a nice surprise."

He swore, punching the seat.

"Watch your language," she warned.

A hard laugh rumbled in Finley's throat. "Do you have any idea the trouble your little stunt has caused me?"

"Dede's a nice girl. If you'll just step outside of yourself long enough you'd realize—"

"Enough!"

The outburst shocked Fiona into silence.

"Who called the hotel pretending to be me?" His voice rose. "Was it dad?" Surely, his dad wasn't involved in this.

He glanced at Sam, caught his sheepish expression in the review mirror. Disgust rattled through his gut. "It was Sam, wasn't it?"

Sam winced. "Sorry, Finley. Your mom said it was for your own good." He tightened his grip on the steering wheel. "She was worried about you spending so much time alone."

"Don't blame, Sam," Fiona said. "I asked him to do it."

Finley gritted his teeth. "I'm well aware on whose shoulders the blame falls. You had no right to interfere in my life that way."

He heard a sniffle, realized his mom was crying. "I just," her voice broke, "I just wish you'd give Dede a chance. She's crazy about you."

"Don't pull the crying card." He rolled his eyes. "It won't work this time. You've gone too far."

"You need a good woman by your side. If you could only find what your dad and I have together."

"I have found it!" he yelled.

The only sound was her sudden intake of breath. "W-what?" she rattled.

He didn't know whether to laugh or cry. "Or at least, I had found it. That is, until you wrecked everything."

"I—I don't understand."

"I found a great woman ... amazing enough to impress even you. I'm crazy about her. She's everything I could ever want and a thousand times more. She's staying at the penthouse suite. You can imagine Sunny's surprise when Dede showed up, claiming that I'd asked her to meet me."

"Oh, no. I didn't mean to mess everything up. I just wanted to help."

"Like you helped at the club?" He laughed humorlessly. "Do me a favor. Stay out of my business."

"I'm so sorry. What can I do to fix this?"

"Let me handle it."

"But—"

"I've gotta go, Mom," he said, ending the call. A second later, his phone buzzed again. It was his mom. He hit the side button to silence it. He looked unseeingly out the window, trying to decide what to do. It only took a few seconds for him to reach a decision. He punched in another number.

His pilot answered. "Hey, Finley, what can I do for you?"

"I need you to get my plane ready. I'm going back to Park City tonight."

Silence.

"Lance, did you hear what I just said?"

"I heard you, but that's not possible."

Bricks settled in Finley's stomach. "Why not?"

"When we landed in Dallas, the mechanic was doing a routine

maintenance check and realized one of the sensors isn't working properly. He ordered the part. It'll come in first thing in the morning. Once it's replaced, we'll be good to go."

"Can we fly without the sensor?"

"Unfortunately, no. Not at night."

This just kept getting better and better. The feeling of urgency that overtook Finley caused his stomach to roil. Somehow, in a way he didn't fully understand, he knew that he had to get to Sunny quickly. "Call around and find me a plane. I don't care what it costs."

"Okey dokey, but it might take a few hours."

"You've got an hour," Finley snapped. "If you can't find something, I'll go to the airport and take the first available commercial flight."

"All right. I'll see what I can do."

Sam looked at him in the rearview mirror. "Am I taking you to the regular airport or the private airfield?"

Not only was Sam his driver but a longtime friend. He glared at Sam's reflection. "I can't believe you were involved in this." The sting of betrayal was acid in his mouth.

"I'm sorry, man. I meant no harm. In your mom's defense, she was only trying to help. A beautiful woman shows up unannounced at your penthouse. I figured you'd be thanking me, know what I mean?" He let out a string of throaty chuckles.

Finley blew out a breath. "Don't do me any more favors," he said dryly. A dull ache pounded across the bridge of his nose. With every second, his apprehension grew. The voice in his head screamed that he needed to get to Sunny as soon as humanly possible. "Take me to the private airport." If he had to, he'd canvas the airport until he found a pilot willing to take him.

He tried calling Sunny again. No answer. Desperation gnawed at his insides. Next, he tried Percy's cell. Hopefully, he'd have some useful information about Nolan Webb. It went to voicemail. Percy normally stayed close to his phone. Something was wrong. He called Percy's home number. His wife answered on the third ring.

"Hi, Joan, this is Finley Landers. I'm sorry to call you in the evening, but I've been trying to reach Percy all day."

A strangled sob came over the line. "Percy's dead."

His heart lurched as he leaned forward, balling his fist. "What?" The words came at him like garbled sounds under water.

"I just found out a couple of hours ago. The police came by to notify me." Her voice broke. "They're calling it suicide, saying he jumped off a building in Vegas."

CHAPTER 13

A loud thump sent Sunny sitting up, her heart pounding. She threw back the covers and jumped out of bed. Had Ian fallen out of his bed? She ran into his room and gaped at what she saw. A terror—swift and paralyzing—iced through her. For a second, she wondered if this was a nightmare. The only light in the room was the shaft of thin moonlight coming from the window. Dr. Clock was standing behind Ian. His face was twisted in an ugly sneer. He had one hand over Ian's mouth and was trying to stick a syringe in his arm with his other hand.

"What're you doing?" she screamed.

Her presence startled the doctor, causing his hand to slip. Ian bit down on it. The doctor yelped and released his hold on Ian, dropping the syringe. Ian's cast went up reflexively and knocked the doctor's glasses off, sending them flying across the room. He let loose a string of curses, flicking his injured hand.

"Help," Ian cried as he dove into Sunny's arms.

Sunny's only thought was to grab Ian and flee.

"Stop or I'll shoot!"

Terror streaked through Sunny when she saw the flash of metal and realized Dr. Clock was holding a gun. This was insane. Somehow, she managed to find her voice as she stepped in front of Ian. "What're you doing here?" Her mind raced to make sense of the situation. Finley had put Dr. Clock on a plane. "How did you get in here?"

He motioned with the gun. "Move away from the door. Now!" he screamed, causing her to flinch. There was a wild tone in the doctor's voice like he might be coming unhinged.

Ian clutched her shirt. "I'm scared," he whimpered.

"It'll be all right," she said to him as much as to herself. She offered up a silent prayer for help. Instinct told her to keep the doctor talking. "What's this all about?"

He barked out a laugh that turned to a snort. "One million dollars." He glanced at the floor, like he was searching for something. Sunny assumed he was looking for the syringe. Then it hit her. *His glasses.* He couldn't see without them. Sunny spied them beside the dresser, about a foot from where she and Ian were standing. If they could get over there, she could step on them.

"Come on, Ian, let's do as the doctor said." She moved toward the dresser.

"Slowly," he ordered.

"Is this about Nolan Webb?"

He let out a grating laugh. "What else?"

"That night with the pillow. You were trying to kill Ian, weren't you?"

He grunted, his expression turning to disdain. "Do you think I'm that stupid? To openly kill the boy?" He wheezed out a nasally laugh, his shoulders moving up and down. "The irony is that now I will have to kill him—both of you." He clicked his tongue. "Maybe Mr. Webb will up the bounty."

A whimper came from Ian's throat as he broke into tears. "I don't wanna die."

"Shut up!" The doctor yelled. "You're a spoiled, idiotic kid!"

"Shh," Sunny said, rubbing Ian's hair.

The glasses were a few inches to the right of her foot. A couple of hard thrusts of her heel was all it would take. She'd break the glasses and then rush at the doctor, try to get the gun away from him. That was their only chance. First, she'd play on his monstrous ego. Get him distracted. "This hotel has top-notch security. How did you get in here?"

He snorted. "Piece of cake. Everyone assumes an intruder will enter through the front door. It's because people are generally stupid. I simply had to rent the room below yours, climb up one story, and come through the patio."

"Won't that incriminate you? The fact that you came back and rented a room?"

He smirked. "Do you really think I'd be stupid enough to rent the room under my real name?"

"So, what was your plan? To kill Ian?" She felt Ian shudder against her. She rubbed a comforting hand over his shoulders. When she went for the doctor, she'd have to push Ian out of the way. Hopefully it wouldn't hurt his broken arm. She couldn't worry about that now. She had to do what was necessary to save them.

"The plan was to take Ian to Mr. Webb." His brows shot down in a V. His face twisted into something hard and ugly, making him look more monster than human. "It would've worked like a charm if the mongrel hadn't woken up and started fighting me." He gave Ian a malicious look.

She forced her tone to go musing. "Let me get this straight. You took the money Finley gave you to keep quiet and then double-crossed us and went to Nolan Webb. Is that how it went down?"

"More or less." He spoke the words with pride like it was a great accomplishment. He looked beside her foot. "Are those my glasses?"

"Huh?" Her heart about stopped. *Crap! What now?*

"Give them to me," he ordered.

Her heart clawed like a caged animal against her chest. "Where are they?"

"Don't play dumb. They're beside your foot."

She forced a laugh. "Oh." She hesitated. "What're you gonna do? Kill us?"

"Yep."

His short answer sent a shudder through her. Was this how it would end? In this dark bedroom with her and Ian huddled together like wretched fugitives? A silent cry wrenched her heart. No, it couldn't end like this! She had to do everything within her power to save Ian. "Let me get the doctor's glasses," she said, extricating Ian from her arms.

"No," Ian protested, trying to hold onto her.

"It'll be okay. Promise." As gently as she could, she pushed Ian away and bent over to retrieve the glasses. "Here." She stepped forward, holding them out. As the doctor went to grab them, she threw them across the room and lunged at him.

She heard Ian's cries as she and the doctor toppled to the floor.

"Run!" she screamed. The doctor held onto the gun with an iron grip. She tried to pry his hand off it as they rolled on the floor, kicking and hitting. Her strength was no match for his. She dug her fingernails into his eye. He swore and punched her across the jaw. The blunt force caused her head to jerk, pain ricocheting through her body. The gun was pointed at her. She tried to push it away. She heard a shot as a searing fire burned a hole through her shoulder. Then she felt liquid oozing out.

"Stop it!" Ian yelled, hysterical.

The doctor pushed her off him, calling her every name in the book as he kicked her viciously in the side. She scuttled back, holding her hand over the bullet wound. A sob wrenched her throat. Ian was still there. He rushed to her side and fell to his knees, clutching her shirt.

The pain was so sharp that she couldn't breathe. Panic engulfed her as a whoosh of lightheadedness overtook her. She fought her way through it. Looked up. Saw the gun pointed at them. She touched Ian's arm. "Don't look," she commanded him. Life was such a beautiful, fragile thing that could be snuffed out in an instant. She'd tried to protect Ian, tried to do right by Lexi, but it was all for naught. "I'm—so—sorry," she whispered.

"Lights out," the doctor sneered.

She heard movement, and then the doctor's surprised gasp.

"Finley!" Ian squealed. He tugged at Sunny's arm. "Finley's here."

Sunny tried to grasp what was happening. Was this a dream? She willed her eyes to focus. Finley had the doctor in a choke hold. The doctor's arms were flailing, the gun still in his hand. A shot was fired.

Ian screamed.

Stars exploded in Sunny's head.

Everything went black.

Then she was drifting.

CHAPTER 14

Finley touched Sunny's hand. It was cold and unresponsive. Her face was covered with an oxygen mask, an IV running into her arm. He looked in horror at the large circle of blood fanned underneath the bandage.

"Excuse me, Mr. Landers," the EMT worker said. "We need to get her into the ambulance."

He swallowed hard, stepping back as the EMTs hurriedly rolled the gurney past him.

"Will Aunt Ashley—Sunny be all right?" Ian asked, his tear-streaked face lifting to Finley's.

Finley forced a smile as he draped an arm around Ian. "Yes, she'll be just fine." Oh, how he hoped that was true! *She'll be okay*, he reassured himself. Sunny had been shot in the shoulder. No vital organs had been hit, but she'd lost a lot of blood. She looked so pale and fragile, lying on the gurney with her eyes closed, going in and out of consciousness.

"I wanna ride in the ambulance with her." Ian thrust out his lower lip, his brows scrunching.

"Me too, but it's better if we drive ourselves to the hospital and meet her there." It was all Finley could do to hang back with Ian, when he wanted more than anything to be by Sunny's side. Sunny would want him to make sure that Ian was looked after by someone he felt comfortable with, and that someone was him.

He stiffened, his eyes narrowing as a group of police officers passed in front of them. They had Dr. Clint Clock in handcuffs, leading him across the foyer and out of the hotel. He tried to catch Clint's eye, but the coward wouldn't even look at him. The good news was that Dr. Clock was the smoking gun. Finley figured the doctor would make a deal with the prosecutor to get a reduced sentence in exchange for him testifying against Nolan Webb. While Finley detested the idea of the doctor escaping the full brunt of the justice owed to him, he wanted Nolan Webb put away for good—for all of the atrocities he'd committed against Sunny, her sister, and Percy. A pit settled in his stomach. If he hadn't sent Percy to investigate Nolan Webb, he'd still be alive right now. Darkness pressed on his chest to the point where it was hard to get a good breath. Although there was nothing Finley could do to make restitution, he'd make sure that Percy's wife never lacked for anything financially the rest of her life.

His thoughts shifted back to Sunny. *Please let her come through this*, he prayed.

Ian tugged on his shirt. "Can we go now?"

"Yes." They'd only gotten a few steps toward the double entrance to the hotel foyer when a woman called out to him. Finley turned, hearing the rapid clicks of stilettos against the floor. Dede rushed toward him. She was wearing only a negligee and silk robe, the untied sash flying out behind her.

She threw her arms around him, giving him a tight hug. "Oh, my gosh! Are you okay?"

"I'm fine," he said curtly, stepping back to put as much distance between them as possible.

Her eyes rounded. "I was so afraid that you'd been shot." She touched his arm, a sultry smile tugging at her lips as she leaned in. "Come up to my room. I can give you a neck massage to help relieve the stress."

"No thanks."

"How about a drink then?"

Finley had the unreasonable urge to laugh in Dede's face. "What're you even doing here?" He shook his head. "You know what? It doesn't matter. I don't have time for this. I need to get to the hospital." He glanced sideways at Ian. "Let's go."

Dede caught his arm. "Wait a minute. I came all this way to see you." Her expression was wounded, eyes pleading. "You're just going to leave me here?"

He grunted. "I never asked you to come here, Dede."

Her face fell. "I thought you'd be happy to see me. Your mother said—"

He held up a hand. "My mother was mistaken. I'm with someone else."

Her voice went soft. "Give me a chance." She stepped closer, her eyes radiating confidence. "The two of us can be so good together."

"I don't think so."

"But I love you."

He rubbed his forehead. The irony of the situation was not lost on him. He chuckled under his breath. "You don't love me, Dede. What you're experiencing is a classic case of The Romeo Effect." A short time ago, he'd been in Dede's shoes. He'd thought his life was over when Emerson dumped him. Now he realized she'd given him the greatest blessing imaginable, the chance to find Sunny. He wished he could somehow bequeath the knowledge of all he'd learned to Dede, but everyone had to learn life's lessons the hard way—through experience.

"Huh?" Dede said dubiously.

"You love the idea of me, or rather, the idea of being in love."

She squared her jaw. "No, that's not true. I love you."

Ian tugged at Finley's shirt. "Can we go now?" he huffed, glaring at Dede. "Finley loves my aunt Sunny, not you." Ian looked at Finley, an open challenge in his eyes. "Isn't that right?"

A surprised laugh rumbled in Finley's throat, mostly because he recognized the truth of Ian's words. "Yes, I love her." The words sent a rush of exultation running through him. "I love her so much that I can hardly wait to get to her side."

Dede's features hardened. "Are you talking about that maid?" She rolled her eyes. "Yes, I know all about her. People in this hotel talk." She grunted. "That woman's not fit to tie your shoelaces."

The hair on Finley's neck rose. "You don't have a clue what you're talking about," he muttered.

Dede let out a malicious laugh. "Oh, I think I have a pretty good idea. Your mother will freak when she hears about this." She folded her arms over her chest, giving him a pointed look. "After your little affair runs its course and you get bored with the maid, don't even think about crawling back to me."

Finley had tried to do this the nice way, but the gloves were now off. "Do you have any idea how ridiculous and desperate you're coming off right now? Showing up here unannounced and pretending that I asked you to come?" He shook his head. "Pathetic."

Dede rocked back, speechless.

"Sunny's the best thing that's ever happened to me. She's got more class in her pinky finger than you've got in your entire body. One thing I've learned is that money can't buy class." He gave her a scathing look. "Unfortunately for you."

Dede's face flushed scarlet.

"Do us both a favor. Go home. Let's go Ian," he barked as he turned on his heel and strode out.

The field was adorned with dainty white clover flowers as far as the eye could see. Sunny looked up at the bright, blue, cloudless sky, trying to get her bearings. They were in the penthouse. The doctor came into Ian's room. She'd been shot, the pain excruciating. Where was Ian? Where was Finley? Her heart clutched as the events came rushing back. The fear, the panic, and finally, the despair at knowing that she didn't have the power to save Ian. *Finley.* Had he come back to help them in the end? Or had she only imagined it?

"Hello, Sis."

She whirled around, surprised to see Lexi standing before her.

"What?" she sputtered, her brain trying to comprehend what was happening. "You can't be here. You're dead."

Lexi only smiled. "You did good, Sis."

Tears rose in Sunny's eyes. "I tried to be a good mom to Ian," she croaked, "but I didn't know how."

"You're doing just fine. You're giving Ian the thing he needs most —love."

An unexpected feeling of warmth flooded over Sunny as she let out a half-laugh. "I do love the stinker, but he gives me a run for my money. I have no idea what to do with him."

She chuckled. "I felt the same way. Take it one day at a time. Before long, you'll get the hang of it. You are enough." Lexi's expression grew serious. "It's finally over."

Sunny tilted her head, not understanding. "What's over?" Fear fluttered in her chest. "Am I dead?" Her heart lurched. She wasn't ready for her life to end.

A wise smile touched Lexi's lips. "I mean, the thing with Nolan. He won't ever be able to hurt you again. You found a good guy. He'll be a good dad to Ian."

"Finley?" Hope swelled inside her. Was it possible? Did Finley truly love her?

"Yes," Lexi said, as if reading her thoughts. "He loves you heart and soul."

A tear rolled down Sunny's cheek. "I miss you."

"I'll always be with you." Lexi's voice seemed to get carried away by the wind, and then she was gone.

"Don't go," Sunny cried, frantically looking around, trying to find her. "Please."

Someone touched her hand. The warmth of the touch seeped into Sunny, overshadowing everything else. She fluttered her eyelids, trying to open her eyes.

"She's waking up," an excited voice said. She knew that voice. Finley. She opened her eyes.

"Hey, beautiful." A broad smile filled Finley's face, tears rising in his eyes as he squeezed her hand. For a moment, all she wanted to do was peer into his golden brown eyes. Then she became more aware of her surroundings as the room came into focus. She looked around at the white, sterile walls and medical equipment. "I'm in the hospital."

"Yes."

She touched her shoulder, the memory of the pain returning.

"Careful," Finley warned, "you don't want to mess up the bandages."

Her stomach tightened. "Ian? Is he okay?"

"He's great. Right here."

She looked over to where Ian was sitting sideways, his legs propped up on the arm of the chair. He gave her a tentative smile, waving. "Hey," he said casually, like they'd only just seen each other a few minutes ago. She thought back to the horrible events that had led them here. "The doctor was going to shoot us." She looked at Finley. "You saved us."

His eyes darkened with emotion. "I was just glad that I got there in time."

"How did you know we were in trouble?"

"I don't know exactly. It was just a strong feeling that I needed to get to you as soon as possible. Then when I discovered that Percy had been killed, the feeling intensified."

Her breath hitched. "What? The investigator?"

He nodded, a shadow crossing his features. "Nolan Webb killed him."

Her heart tightened. "Oh, no. I'm so sorry."

"Me too." His mouth formed a tight line.

"What about the doctor?"

"He was arrested." Finley's eyes narrowed. "And if I have anything to say about it, he'll be put behind bars a long time."

She sighed. "Good." Then she thought of something else. "What about Nolan Webb?"

A fierce look came into Finley's eyes. "He'll never be able to hurt you again."

The dream came rushing back, causing Sunny's pulse to increase. "What do you mean?"

"The police went to arrest him. Nolan pulled a gun. A shootout took place, and Nolan was killed."

Her head began to spin. The dream. It was a dream, wasn't it? She thought of something else Lexi said as she gazed into Finley's eyes. "You love me heart and soul."

He laughed in surprise, rubbing his thumb in circles over her hand. "Actually, I do."

Tears misted her eyes. "I love you too."

He rewarded her with a gargantuan smile. "It works nicely, doesn't it? The two of us were meant for each other."

"Yes," she agreed, a feeling of contentment coming over her. That only lasted for a second, however. She shook her head, her brows furrowing. "But wait. What about the other woman?"

"Dede?"

"Yeah." She was sure her distaste for the spoiled debutante was written all over her face. She eyed Finley. He'd better have a darn good explanation for all that had occurred.

Finley chuckled nervously. "That was a big misunderstanding. Something my mom orchestrated."

She lifted an eyebrow, not ready to let him off the hook. "Drake said you called and told him Dede was coming."

"My mom got her driver to pretend to be me."

Sunny made a face. "I take it that means she doesn't like me very much if she went to all that trouble to get you together with someone else." She shouldn't be surprised, but it still stung to know that Finley's mom didn't approve of her. The woman hadn't even met her yet, and she was already casting judgment.

Finley's eyes sparkled, a smile tugging at his lips.

She frowned. "What?"

"You have no idea how tempting it is to put The Romeo and Juliet Effect into practice right now."

"Huh?" Normally, she would've gotten his joke instantly, but her brain was still a little fuzzy.

"You know, to make our love for one another even stronger in the face of parental opposition."

"You're terrible," she responded, but couldn't help grinning.

He laughed. "The truth is, my mom didn't even realize that you existed when she tried to fix me up with Dede."

"Oh." She didn't know if that was a good or bad thing.

"Don't worry," he assured her, "she and my dad know about you now." He gave her a confident smile. "I promise you. My mom's going to love you as much as I do."

The moment slowed as he leaned in to kiss her. Electricity zinged through her when their lips touched.

"Ew, gross." Ian made a gagging sound, sticking his finger in his throat.

Sunny and Finley pulled apart, both laughing.

Finley glanced at him. "Trust me, Bud, you won't think it's gross a few years from now."

"Get a room," Ian boomed.

Sunny's eyes widened as she gasped. She shot Ian a sharp look. "Excuse me?"

Ian gave her a sheepish expression, his face reddening. "Sorry."

It occurred to Sunny that Ian probably didn't even have a clue what he was talking about. He was most likely repeating something he'd heard on TV. She thought of what Lexi said in the dream about taking the parenting thing one day at a time. *I am enough*, she repeated mentally.

Finley leaned back in, his eyes dancing "Ian, you'd better close your eyes, Bud, because I'm about to give your aunt a long, thorough kiss that would put Romeo to shame."

Sunny laughed, shivers of anticipation dancing down her spine. "Is that so? That's a pretty lofty statement, Mr. Landers." Her breath came faster, her lips parting. She felt his warm breath on her face, knew it wouldn't take much for her to get completely lost in the feel of his lips.

"One that I'm prepared to uphold today and forever, for the rest of our lives," Finley uttered, his lips taking hers.

EPILOGUE

Six months later ...

Butterflies swarmed in Sunny's stomach as she faced the wide red ribbon tied across the front entrance of the newly renovated Belmont Hotel. A throng of reporters were gathered around them, snapping pictures of everything that moved.

"You've got this," Finley whispered in her ear, giving her hand a reassuring squeeze. She felt her ridiculously large, diamond engagement ring move into the side of her finger. Even though Sunny told Finley she didn't want a conspicuous ring, he insisted on getting her the very best. A burst of elation swelled through her as she glanced sideways at him. His eyes sparkled as he gave her an intimate smile. For a moment, everyone else faded away, and it was just the two of them. "I love you."

His eyes caressed hers. "I love you back."

Regardless of how the ribbon cutting and open house went tonight, Sunny was happy. She glanced at Ian who was standing beside Finley. He gave her a large smile and hearty thumbs up. No longer was she waiting for disaster to befall her. She was learning to live in the moment. Life was a gift, and she intended to live it fully, holding nothing back.

Her shoulder recovery had been tough, but Finley stayed right by her side, nursing her back to full health. In an unexpected turn of events, Sunny's injury had brought her closer to Ian. It made him feel like he wasn't the only one who was incapacitated. They recovered together. Luckily, they were both now back to normal ... well, as normal as the two of them could possibly be. She chuckled to herself at the thought.

After the wedding, Finley was determined to take Sunny and Ian to Europe for a few months, insisting that it was a perfect set-up because Ian was homeschooled. Afterwards, the plan was for them to set up their primary residence in Dallas but get a vacation home in Park City.

Drake cleared his throat and straightened to his full height as he ran a hand over his tux coat. "It's with great pleasure that we present our newly renovated hotel." Pride shone in his eyes as he motioned at Sunny. "The chief designer on the project is our very own Miss Sunny Day."

Applause broke out amongst the group as he cut the ribbon with giant scissors.

As people filed into the hotel, Kenton Landers touched her arm. "Well done."

"Thank you. I'm glad you like the hotel," Sunny said.

"The hotel is nice," he said absently, touching his bowtie. "But what I meant is that I'm glad you're a part of our lives." He looked at Finley. "You've given my son everything a father could ever hope for, something that money could never buy."

Emotion rose in her throat as she smiled. "Thank you."

Fiona caught up with Sunny inside the foyer. She pursed her lips, her gaze encompassing the foyer. "You know," she mused, her finger going to her lips. "Any woman who can pull together something of this magnitude has got to be worth her salt." She gave Sunny an appraising look, her lips curving into a smile.

Sunny grinned. "Thanks, Fiona." That was the closest thing to a compliment she'd ever received from Fiona Landers. Despite Fiona's guarded demeanor, Sunny could tell she was a good person at heart.

"You know," Sunny drawled in the same tone Fiona had used, "any woman who can raise a son as amazing as Finley has got to be worth her salt." She cut her eyes at her future mother-in-law, waiting for a response.

Fiona laughed in surprise, touching her short hair. "You know what? I think the two of us are going to get along just fine," she winked as she sauntered away to mingle with the other guests.

Arms encircled Sunny from behind. "How's the most beautiful woman in the room?" Finley murmured in her ear. He planted a string of light kisses along her neck. She closed her eyes, savoring the moment.

"Great," she hummed, turning to face him.

His eyes moved over her in a slow, leisurely way that got her blood pumping faster. "So, after this is over, I thought we might check out the new hot tub." He pumped his eyebrows, a goofy grin spilling over his lips.

She laughed. "Sounds like a date."

A crash from the other side of the room commanded their attention. They looked at the table where the water dispensers and glasses were located. Ian had fallen over the table and knocked over a stack of drinking glasses.

"Oh, no." Sunny clutched her throat.

All eyes turned to Ian as he stood. He turned, wide-eyed, toward Sunny and Finley. A sheepish grin overtook his face as he held up his hands. "I'm okay," he announced.

This brought a few amused chuckles from the guests as Drake rushed to clean up the broken glass.

Sunny moved to go to Ian's side, but Finley touched her arm. "I've got this."

She shook her head. "Never a dull moment," she lamented.

He winked, giving her a crooked smile. "I wouldn't have it any other way."

As the guests resumed their conversations, Sunny thought she caught a trace of Lexi's amused laughter in the air, prompting her to stop taking herself too seriously, to enjoy life. She couldn't help but smile as she watched Finley ruffle Ian's hair and pat him on the back. "I am enough," she said to herself.

This was enough—more than she could've ever hoped for. As she looked at the man and boy she loved more than anything in the world. Her heart swelled larger than Texas.

Tears rose in her eyes, and she felt so incredibly blessed.

YOUR FREE BOOK AWAITS ...

Hey there, thanks for taking the time to read *The Jilted Billionaire Groom*. If you enjoyed it, please take a minute to give me a review on Amazon. I really appreciate your feedback, as I depend largely on word of mouth to promote my books.

The Jilted Billionaire Groom is a stand-alone novel, but you'll also love other books in Jennifer's Texas Titan Romance Series.

The Persistent Groom

The Ghost Groom

The Hometown Groom

The Jilted Billionaire Groom

The Impossible Groom

To receive updates when more of my books are coming out, sign up for my newsletter at http://jenniferyoungblood.com/

If you sign up for my newsletter, I'll give you one of my books, Beastly Charm: A contemporary retelling of beauty & the beast, for FREE. Plus, you'll get information on discounts and other freebies. For more information, visit:

http://bit.ly/freebookjenniferyoungblood

Your free book awaits …

BOOKS BY JENNIFER YOUNGBLOOD:

Check out Jennifer's Amazon Page:
http://bit.ly/jenniferyoungblood

Georgia Patriots Romance
The Hot Headed Patriot
The Twelfth Hour Patriot

O'Brien Family Romance
The Impossible Groom (Chas O'Brien)
The Twelfth Hour Patriot (McKenna O'Brien)
Rewriting Christmas (A Novella)
Yours By Christmas (Park City Firefighter Romance)
Her Crazy Rich Fake Fiancé

Navy SEAL Romance
The Resolved Warrior
The Reckless Warrior
The Diehard Warrior

The Jane Austen Pact

Seeking Mr. Perfect

Texas Titan Romances

The Hometown Groom

The Persistent Groom

The Ghost Groom

The Jilted Billionaire Groom

The Impossible Groom

The Perfect Catch (Last Play Series)

Hawaii Billionaire Series

Love Him or Lose Him

Love on the Rocks

Love on the Rebound

Love at the Ocean Breeze

Love Changes Everything

Loving the Movie Star

Love Under Fire (A Companion book to the Hawaii Billionaire Series)

Kisses and Commitment Series

How to See With Your Heart

Angel Matchmaker Series

Kisses Over Candlelight

The Cowboy and the Billionaire's Daughter

Romantic Thrillers

False Identity

False Trust

Promise Me Love

Burned

Contemporary Romance

Beastly Charm

Fairytale Retellings (The Grimm Laws Series)
    Banish My Heart **(This book is FREE)**
    The Magic in Me
    Under Your Spell
    A Love So True

Southern Romance
    Livin' in High Cotton
    Recipe for Love

The Second Chance Series
    Forgive Me (Book 1)
    Love Me (Book 2)

Short Stories
    The Southern Fried Fix

ABOUT JENNIFER YOUNGBLOOD

Jennifer loves reading and writing clean romance. She believes that happily ever after is not just for stories. Jennifer enjoys interior design, rollerblading, clogging, jogging, and chocolate. In Jennifer's opinion there are few ills that can't be solved with a warm brownie and scoop of vanilla-bean ice cream.

Jennifer grew up in rural Alabama and loved living in a town where "everybody knows everybody." Her love for writing began as a young teenager when she wrote stories for her high school English teacher to critique.

Jennifer has BA in English and Social Sciences from Brigham Young University where she served as Miss BYU Hawaii. Before becoming an author, she worked as the owner and editor of a monthly newspaper named *The Senior Times*.

She now lives in the Rocky Mountains with her family and spends her time writing and doing all of the wonderful things that make up the life of a busy wife and mother.

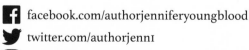

facebook.com/authorjenniferyoungblood
twitter.com/authorjennı
instagram.com/authorjenniferyoungblood